May hope for the
future protect us

JOURNEY THROUGH FOLDING-SPACE

No hope for the human race.
No hope for the planet.
What time is it?

KEITH RADMALL

Ordering Information:

Prime Seven Media
518 Landmann St.
Tomah City, WI 54660

Printed in the United States of America

TABLE OF CONTENTS

Part One

Time Traveller

Part Two

Dialogues

Part Three

Coronavirus

Part Four

Covid-19

TIME TRAVELLER

TIME TRAVEL

Man washed up
on beach.

Wizard looking
into an orb.

Diary of a time traveller

Fighter plane with
exploding tug boat.

Stone age man
holding club.

Believe, then don't believe.
Believe or don't believe.

Changes in
civilisation.

Mountain
scenery.

Right to life.

War is war.

Changes in
oneself.

Outer limits,
Outer space,
Out of time.

Sorrow of us all.

Machine fix.

DIARY OF A TIME TRAVELLER

Though I walk through the valley of
Death, I shall fear no evil

Time Traveller

I shall respect all that is
around me because it is
theirs, not mine

There are no expectations in time travel
Because every place you come to is different.

Before time = Trip
Present time = Invisible time
Future time = Vision

Time Travel

Time travel = Thought
Time traveller = Experience
Time machine = Objective

Past + Relic + Ancestry

=

Dead on time.

REASSURANCE IN TIME

Name:

First Name:

Last Name:

Date of Birth:

Place of Birth:

Home Address:

Phone Number:

E-mail Address:

National Insurance Number:

License Number:

Qualifications:

Training:

Hobbies:

Activities:

Certificates:

Work Experience:

WAR OF CROWNS

With the end of the Roman occupation, the kingdoms of Britain are beginning to arise again. The whispers are the only way to hear news from across the land. The people are beginning to wonder who will rule the lands. There is King Equar of Cornwall, whose doctrine is, 'What's yours is mine; you can have the rest.' There is King Burr of Middle Earth, whose belief is, 'Give peace a chance; I shall have the rest.' Also thought of as a contender is King Auar of the north, whose belief is, 'You can keep your kingdom, but you must pay retribution once a year to me.'

The war breaks out between King Equar and King Burr, with king Equar sweeping across the south lands. He punches northwards but is stopped at the northlands border. With trouble in the Welsh highlands and King Burr retreating to the northern corner for a final stand, King Auar makes his move and attacks from two sides.

King Equar is pushed back; facing defeat, he retreats to his stronghold, waiting for an onslaught that never came. With King Burr's forces weakened by seven years of non-stop battle and King Auar not willing to weaken his force by spreading them out across the land, the final outcome was, 'Let us see what happens through experience,' knowing whoever broke would face certain death.

F. T. Note: The final outcome is written in history, with King Arthur and the Knights of the Round Table being put to the sword.

THE BLACKSMITH

It is five years since the Romans were thrown out of Britain. I'm working as a blacksmith on the northern road which separates the north from London in the south. I have a fine smithy with all kinds of weaponry on the wall. There is an iron stove for smelting and an anvil for shoeing horses and tapping iron.

The heads of captured and killed Romans line the road, with a few cages spread between them which hold the skeleton remains of traitors and collaborators.

I am working at my anvil for some person who has gone to the inn across the road. His horse threw a shoe, and I have been offered a half-crown by him if I can do it right away. A stranger approaches carrying a stick with a green glass bubble on it. His coat is made of red hide and has many feathers on the shoulders of it.

The stranger asks if he is on the right road to London. I answer yes. Then I say, 'But there is an inn across the road, and you look like you need some rest.'

The stranger answers, 'Alas, I am on the way to London to make solace with the future.'

As he is walking away I wonder if he knew I knew he was the wizard Merlin. I think then what will happen to this adventurous land when a reject from a lost land gets together with the rejects of a dammed land.

F. T. Note: Careful how you interpret what others say to you.

THE MISSION

I am but a child. I am looking through a hole in the wall. It is a stone shack with a fireplace on the left side of the wall. The roof is made of reeds. Every night, I am placed in my blanket of white greyish downing, and I look up through the hole and see a bright single star. Then one night, a flash of light passes by near the star. I wonder what it is. As the years pass, I am standing with my father outside our home. Then suddenly there is a great thundering sound, and over the hillside comes riding a vast army. As they get closer, they slow down and stop within twelve feet of us. A man on a white horse wearing golden armour, a cloak, and a crown trots slowly forward.

I grab my father's trouser leg tightly. Then the man on the horse says, 'I am a king, so I am going to take all your harvest from the past year. Where is it?'

My father answers, 'In the shed over yonder hillside.'

The man on the horse hands my father a pouch with twelve golden coins in it and says, 'Thank you.' Then the vast army rides off.

Many years have passed. I am now grown-up. I am getting my horse ready to go to town to buy reebling from the passing merchant.

Then suddenly I awaken as if from a dream. I am adrift at sea, holding on to a piece of wood from a ship. As my mind clears, I look around and see nothing but the sea. As the hours pass, I spot land, and by struggling in the sea and holding onto the piece of wood, I eventually reach land. After a short rest to dry my clothes and gather my senses, I make my way inland. I meet a flour mill trader who is selling his wares from Portsmouth to Birmingham.

THE MISSION #2

I meet him east of Portsmouth. Luckily, he is a good man and offers me a place to rest and food for help with his journey. I tell him I accept, and for the next three months, I am stopping, selling, and buying between Portsmouth and Birmingham. At journey's end, I get paid one pound eighteen shilling, with which I buy a horse, a pistol, and new clothes.

Then I ride to a place called the Dark Skull Tavern on the London road. My adventure starts there. I become a highwayman and gain a reputation, with a hundred-pound bounty on my head. On one of my excursions, I hold up a stagecoach, and inside is a beautiful lady wearing a very beautiful diamond necklace with a large green sapphire as its centrepiece. I take the necklace from around her neck plus other trinkets in her possession.

I return to the Dark Skull Tavern, where I can trade the trinkets. I sell all but the glittering necklace piece, which I keep for some reason.

Then one night at the tavern, soldiers burst in. Three of us manage to escape, and we decide to go to the port of London and lie low. After a drunken night by the ships, I look up and see what that piece of wood was from that helped to save me. It was from a bird's nest, where the lookout would watch for enemy ships and dangers while at sea. Then I see a shooting star pass by it, making it seem to glow. I find an old, half-sunken boat with its bird's nest partly intact and take the part's bird nest with me to the inn where I am residing.

A few days later in a tavern, at the dock, I see a man with a chart. I ask him about it, and he says it was one of the first known maps of the world. There and then, I know I have to have it. After a few drinks and some haggling, in which the seller looks like he is getting the better part of the deal, I buy the map from him for seven pounds, ten shillings.

THE MISSION #3

Back at my place of residence, I place the map on the table. Then I place the partial bird's nest next to the window. Just before dawn, I place the green emerald necklace on the centre top of the half bird's nest. As the sun goes down and the moon rises, a light shines on the map. There are two guiding points reaching out to places in Japan, and those places are Hiroshima and Nagasaki. As I look at the map, everything gets blurry.

The next thing I remember, it is 1945, and I am jumping out of an airplane. I look up to see my parachute. As soon as I touch down, I bury my parachute in the ground. Then after donning my Japanese clothes and mask, I make my way towards Hiroshima using my map references. After a week of walking, I reach the Duck Cafe in central Hiroshima and order a cup of tea. There, sitting in a booth four booths ahead and to the right of me is Jengy. Not wanting to cause suspicion, I drink my tea and leave. *So far, everything is going to plan*, I think as I make my way down the coast to my final destination, Nagasaki.

I climb a hill just outside Nagasaki. I take an elevator, which takes me deep underground. I make myself busy for the final countdown.

I mix the different degrees of vegetation that give an elixir of life in Japan. Then I boil it to create a liquid form for two syringes. I let it cool down and then place it in the syringes. As I put them safely in the drawer, I think of the first nuclear bomb hitting Hiroshima. On the fourth day, I rise from what feels like a sea of tears. I open the draw and gently put the two syringes into my utility belt. I prepare for the inevitable. I press the button, and the door to the elevator opens. I can feel the energy of the nuclear warhead as it heads for the surface. When I reach ground level, I see nothing but bleakness.

THE MISSION #4

I start running towards it. As I pass through the ashes of destruction, I grab my first syringe and give it to a hardly recognisable lady. Then while moving on towards the beachfront, I give a small boy child the other syringe.

This time, I stop and watch as the aura of life, like a riptide, starts spreading. I know that the essence of evil has a head start, but there is no stopping the aura of the plant because there is nothing to stand in its way as it picks up speed.

Jengy comes screaming wildly out of the coffee shop as the bomb falls, firing his guns and screaming, 'As I die a warrior, you shall die a thousand deaths.'

I make my way to the beachfront just outside the blast zone. On reaching the beachfront I turn back into a human form. I then sit down in the sand, take the cyanide pill from my tin, and swallow it. I then lie back in the sand to die.

A tugboat arrives and picks me up. It carries me and lays me on one of the shelf seats.

Speaking Russian, a man says, 'Who are you? What are you doing?' With foam coming from my mouth, I try to say, 'Your bullshit.'

Then a Japanese fighter plane comes flying at us, firing. It must hit the gasoline tank because then is a mighty explosion.

F. T. Note: It's not finding the truth that matters. It's how far you will go to find the truth.

IN BETWEEN BELIEFS

What is an eclipse
if not a memory?

Where is the future
if it is in the past?

To the human mind,
it's on the tip of your tongue.

To the all-seeing eye,
what you see is what you get.

In the beginning, there was man;
in the future, there was the rest of man.

In the past, there were dinosaurs;
in the future, there were creatures of Earth.

All the treasures of the planet
are where they are there.

THE FUTURIST

To become a reader of the future, you must
be pure of heart and mind.

There are three steps you have to learn.

1. Become knowledgeable about what is happening in the world.

2. Learn how to separate the bit truth from psychotic ramblings.

3. Know when to throw your mind.

When you learn the three steps, and if successful in
your first attempt, you will become overwhelmed
with the feeling you have been truly gifted.

F. T. Note: Use caution if you ever decide
to coagulate the three moves.

Tread warily and combine stealth and secrecy while gambling.

Remember, once the gift is gone, it's gone forever.

MEMORIES OF A TIME TRAVELLER

Dear Heights: What they were.
There were so few when I first saw it; now there are so many.

It is easy when you see it.
It is so hard when you're not sure.

Timid Growth:

Made it so unbelievable is true.

I have not much time;

I am passing through a void.

If you want to make it, you must align yourself to the four elements.

Then enhance your being to your immediate
surroundings. Then you might make it.

Wait, keep waiting, wait for it.
Wow, look at that.

F. T. Note: Now you see it, now you don't!
Once it was, now it is.

Timeline Counter: She threw my notebook
away because she was coming apart,
but I forgive her.

P. S: I think who ever finds the notebook will try to
trick me between falsehood and immunology.

STRANGE EXPERIENCE

I was high up in the mountainous region of Europe called the Alps. It was very wintery, and I wondered whether a ride would come along or whether I would have to use my initiative. Luckily, I managed to flag a lift of a truck; the driver spoke little English. I see we were very high in the mountains because the city down below looked like a few specks of light. We were going along, and then the driver signalled that the brakes were failing. Then he fell asleep, so I grabbed the steering wheel. As we picked up speed, I manoeuvred the sleeping man into the passenger seat. I shifted the gear slowly down to first from eighteen. Our speed quickly went from 85 to 140 kilometres per hour. While I tried to buffer the speed against the mountainside, I took my foot away from the brake pedal. I released the accelerator also and used only the hand brake.

We were swerving about, but there was nothing else I could do. I knew if I pulled hard on the hand brake, I might lock up the wheels, and we would be doomed. I needed nature to play its part, hoping the change in air density at sea level would create air pressure on the brakes. We came hurtling out of the mountains, and I caught site of a rest stop to my right. I slowly pressed the brake pedal, and with a yuk and an auk, the truck began to slow down. The truck driver was still sleeping, so I drove on until we reached Vienna. The road went in to directions, one towards Italy and the other towards Germany.

I pulled into a lay-by, switched off the engine, and put the driver in the driving seat. He woke and indicated he was going towards Italy. I was going the other way, so we parted company.

F. T. Note: It's good to be good to others; it makes you feel good inside.

RECURRING NIGHTMARE

I am underwater, and I open my eyes, I feel trapped and cannot move. I am dressed in diving gear. I survey my surroundings and see a big sunken boat. It looks like its mast is across my legs, keeping me pinned on the seabed. There is tangled rope and debris all around me. I try desperately to move it, but I cannot. I check how much air I have left in my tank: it reads just over four and a half minutes. I try desperately to get free, but it will not budge.

Things are getting desperate. I check my air again and have just over two and a half minutes. Then an idea comes to me, and I start digging out the sand from underneath me. It works, and there is movement, so I dig frantically. I manage to slide out from under the mast, and I move rope and debris away so I don't get tangled in it. I stand up, release my weight belt, and inflate my bouncy vest. I start for the surface while checking my depth gauge, which reads thirty meters and a half a minute of air. I start moving quicker, and then I see light on the surface of the water. I check the gauge: I have twenty seconds of air left.

I quickly undo my air tank strap and, with ten seconds of air left, take a deep breath in and then discard the tank and breathing apparatus. I break the surface and gasp for air.

I look around and am in a cove. The nearest land is about 125 yards away. I swim towards it, reach the beach, and collapse on it, exhausted.

F. T. Note: The aura of the nightmare changes into something trying to eat your face from within, never quite making it. Then it decimates into nothingness.

WAR CHILD

Definition: A war child is a baby born in a country ravaged by the turmoil and terror of war.

I watched as the American tried to manipulate the rest of the world so the masses would believe it was they, not them, who instigated the conflict in Korea.

I listened as the American bragged about drugs and beer during the Vietnam War; alas, there was loss.

I switched on the television as America fired the first shots to begin the destruction of Persia and thus the end of Western influence in the area.

There are three things running around in your mind at the moment.

1) When will the Persian conflict end?

2) Where will the next big war happen?

3) What will be the next big atrocity to hit America?

The war child will grow up with great power, but do not worry, Mr. President, Dictator, Prime Minister. If you are willing to accept the consequences of your actions, you will be fine.

DEATH INCARNATE

A foetus is like a kaleidoscope, a silhouette forming.

If that formatting is interrupted in any way, it is like an earthquake.

After the fact, it tries to repair any damage if possible.

But because of it, the mirage of 'all right now' is shown with a shadow effect.

Then comes birth with a three-minute, twenty-seven-second dead time.

Then someone notices signs of life, retrieved from the dead basket.

What I see is a haze of blood and carnage.

Then as life goes on, every time the future looks good, I was hit with a surge of immense pain, sometimes lasting until I blacked out. Once past the prime of life, a lower level of pain became a constant reminder of what I missed out on.

F. T. Note: Don't get trapped between nothingness and the future. All you are gifted with is loneliness and sadness.

BIRD IN FLIGHT

Beginning of time:

Tap … Tap … Tap … Tap … Tap … Tap …

Tap … Tap … Tap … Tap … Tap … Tap …

Tap … Tap … Tap … Tap … Tap … Tap …

Tap … Tap … Tap … Tap … Tap … Tap …

Tap … Tap … Tap … Tap … Tap … Tap …

Tap … Tap … Tap … Tap … Tap … Tap …

Beginning of life!

F. T. Note: The greatest happening ever.

SPIRITUAL RENAISSANCE

What is a spirit? When you engulf the final thought before you are dead, you enhance the spirit world.

Example: I am on an expanse of grassland, and it is a clear day. I look up into the sky. I see in the distance something coming down towards me. I walk in the direction in which I believe it will land, and I feel a confrontation coming on. Then on a hilly mound of grass before me is a giant dragon. It is red in colour with big golden claws. It lets out a great roar which seems to go on forever. Not wanting to get struck by one of its claws, I turn and start walking away. I turn and watch as the dragon, with a swoosh, starts circling in the sky until I cannot see it. While walking on, I realise what I was trying to say. I chose the path; I must finish the journey. My last thought is, 'Maybe I am wrong. Maybe it isn't.'

P. T. Note: What I saw, was it

> Something from another place?
> Something that knew me?
> An image of myself in another time?

F. T. Note: One thing is for sure: know the answer to these questions. Then otherworldly beings will be knocking on earth's door.

HUMAN BEINGS

I decided when I first knew of the phenomenon, I would let it develop until I found out as much as I could about it. When I thought I was ready, I enhanced my nearest surroundings. Then I opened the door to the Orbital by putting my hand on it. Inside, after deciding where to go, I set the solaric to show 'where humans took their first steps' on the screen and pressed the button. When the screen showed I had arrived, I opened the door. I found myself in a swamp-like area, and after a small walk, I could see a clearing. There were a few people walking around unclothed, and beyond there was a rock face that looked like it had caves in it.

I went back to the Orbital, removed my clothes, and went to mingle. Except for the odd look, it went OK. Eventually, I ending up with a group sitting around. The language was easy to understand, with *Uh* and *Guh* being about it. They communicated through signing and expressions, and they looked like they had to do something.

There came a time when there were only three of us, so with a *Guh*, I got up to leave. As I turned away from the other two, I felt I was clubbed on the head. When I awoke, it felt like a surge of heat was running through me, as if I had been skewered.

The intensity of the heat seemed to go higher and higher. The next thing I remembered was leaning against the Orbital and feeling very rough. I opened the door and climbed in. After clicking the door closed with what felt like the last drop of energy inside me, I set off the solaric to show 'from whence I came' on the screen.

I pressed the button.

Once the screen indicated I had arrived, I put on my clothes and opened the door. Outside, after recognising my surroundings, I turned and watched as the Orbital disappeared before my eyes. I then cautiously went on my way.

I discovered I had been gone for seven days, and nobody realised I had left.

F. T. Note: A proven fact is if you forge a lifeline in another time, all knowledge of your past is eradicated.

THIS IS IT

Fading into the recesses of my mind is, 'Picking up the pieces of my broken life.' Then rushing through my mind is, 'This is it.' I climb the eleven levels to the flat and then open the door. I look around, deciding where to do it. The next day, I am looking around the kitchen, and nobody is in there. I climb on the outside windowsill. I then dive off it towards the ground below, and my head hits the pathway. Then I am standing hidden in the bushes, am looking at what looks like a bewildered myself. I decide to wait a while, but then I have a thought. I am soon climbing up the stairs to the flat.

I am standing in a small field surrounded by a metal fence. I want to see how quickly I can get from one position to a given point. I enhance myself and then choose a point about twenty-five feet ahead of me. I throw my mind, emphasising the position ahead of me. Then within the blink of an eye, I am standing in that position and looking back where I was. I now want to see whether I can move quickly over long distance. I choose a bus stop on one side of town and a bus stop I know on the other side of town. After checking them out, a week later I go to the first bus stop; there is nobody else there. I enhance myself, fix on the location of the other bus stop, and then throw my mind. It works: in the blink of an eye, I am standing at the other bus stop with my back to whence I came. There is a lady standing at the bus stop with her back to me. When she turns, she sees and looks startled. I say sorry. I do not want to catch the bus, so I make as if I have forgotten something and cross the road.

The next time, I want to know what speed I could reach. While standing at the gateway to the prairies in eastern Canada, I enhance myself, think about speed, and throw my mind. I feel instantly the mass of speed. Upon arriving at the gateway to the Rocky Mountains in the west, I look at my watch and calculate. I reached a speed of 1.3 billion miles per hour.

Faintly in my mind, I think I shall return to this place. On returning, it is very cold with the wind howling. The temperature is twenty-seven below zero. I lie down on the snow thinking, *Once I was, now I am where I was*, and then I fall asleep. Exactly three weeks later, I awake. The snow is thick, the wind is howling, and the temperature is fifty degrees below zero. I feel reinvigorated and have enough energy to finish my journey.

F. T. Note: I am a mere child,

        I am but a boy,

           I am a teenager.

INDIAN GIVER

I am above South America in the western hemisphere, which will come to be known as the new world. I have decided to take a journey as an Indian.

I step out of the Orbital holding the thought, *I was, I am*. Next, I am with a group of us deep in the forest of South America. We are sitting around a campfire and absorbing our spirit world for what is to come.

It is a strange, powerful sensation full of trepidation and blood thirst. Then after standing, like ghosts, we go our separate ways.

Next, I am in North America. I enter a cave and sit down by one of the others. We all wear different attire, but it is all Indian mystic. We look at each other and know when we leave the cave, we shall die. While looking straight ahead, we summon our darkest spirit, and then we all feel at peace with ourselves. Upon rising, we look at each other and utter one word, *chyou*, meaning goodbye. We clench each other's arms and depart first in, first out.

Next, I am looking at soldiers shooting as I go around them, firing my arrows. My blood is rushing, then I feel a twinge on my left cheek, and then the vision is no more.

I am now standing alone, out in the wilderness of Atowou, better known as the Arctic North. After sitting down, I know my Indian journey is coming to an end. I close my eyes and imagine going deeper into an abyss. I think, *I am, I was*.

As I touch the Orbital, the door opens. I step inside, and the door closes. I set the latch and then am gone.

F. T. Note: A piece of hope,
        A piece of hell,
            A piece of nothingness.

THE BIG SHIP

I arrived in 1932, and down below was the Atlantic Ocean. A ship floated on the ocean. I move the screen so I could decipher the name on the ship. The name read *Titanic*. I decided to have myself a cruise and set the Orbital on the aft of the ship. I ensured I had money and left the Orbital in an invisible state.

I coerced a cabin from one of the deck hands for £150, which was very expensive for essentially a storage unit.

I had five fantastic days on board a ship that looked more like a stately home. The meals were exquisite, as was the entertainment. I would like to thank the steward for taking care of me, which cost me twenty-five pounds a pop.

It was an eerie moment when the ship swiped the iceberg. It was a cold, gloomy night. I observed a slow transition of sombre emergence heading towards full-blown worry. I could do nothing, but I was not going to leave them. I helped people lost in the aisles to reach the demarcation lifeboats. I found a small cabin five decks down and, until the darkest hour, gave directions to help find safety. In the last few moments before the ship broke in two and sank, there was an older gentleman, a young lady, and two young children, a boy of four and his sister of seven. I hustled them into the cabin and then closed the door. It was like a floating sensation as the ship sank and creaked downwards. The sea rushing in was like a quiet thunder. As the four hearts sat on the sofa and I sat on a chair, we looked at each other, slowly looking like ghosts preparing for the spirit world.

I broke the silence by trying to cheer everyone up: 'We're all off on a new adventure.'

After seventeen minutes, we touched the bottom of the sea. We talked to each other about our lives. The older gentleman said how he dealt in car parts. The young lady was on her honeymoon, and the children were on holiday with their parents. I said I travelled and had seen many wonderous places.

The next four minutes were heartbreaking as the old man, then the young lady, then the boy, then the girl passed away as if falling asleep.

I changed to my original form and hoped for their spirits to find them. I then stood up, went to the door, and opened it. As the sea rushed in, I thought, *The sea shall have not them.*

I swam to the Orbital, which was floating on the surface. I clambered inside and set the solaric to the outer ionosphere. I could not hold my emotions any longer and cried for what felt like hours.

TIME TRAVEL TRIVIA

I lie back in a park. It is a nice sunny day, and there is nobody else around. Then someone else arrives and sits down about twelve feet away from me. I say to him, 'I know why you are here.'

He says, 'And why is that?'

I say to him, 'You want to know what hell incarnate is.'

He says, 'Then show me.'

I say, 'OK, but you must first throw your mind, and if you don't, I won't show you.' I wait a bit and then say, 'Have you done it?'

He says yes, so I look into his face and say, 'No, you haven't. You're lying to me, so I won't show you.'

He starts hassling me about it, so I tell him to meet me here in three days at twelve thirty.

In three days, he returns at twelve thirty. I say, 'Are you ready?' He says yes. I know he is because of how serious he looks. I tell him to throw his mind, and then I flick my finger at him. He falls back to the ground. I then say, 'What is wrong? Tell me all.'

First he says, 'My lungs—I can't breathe. they're burning up.' Then he says, 'I can't hear anything—my ears are exploding.' Then with an agonising expression, he adds, 'I can't see.'

I reply, 'Don't worry; you will be fine.' He falls asleep. I sit down next to him, and after five minutes, thirty-two seconds, he wakes and slowly gets to his feet. I stand and say, 'Are you feeling OK?' When he says yes, I say, 'Good,' and walk away.

I keep seeing empty white light all around me. Each time it comes about, I try to walk a bit farther to reach the other side. Nothing seems to be working, so I devise a plan of motion detection, realising it must be the right moment.

I have been caught in a void for so long now. I really want to know what was on the other side. So the next time the void of white light emptiness comes about, I throw my mind in a divided transcript of the four elements. Then with a mitigation of satisfaction, I break through and walk out of the void and into a rolling hillside landscape.

I am just pleased it was not my downfall.

F. T. Note: There are many different landscapes out there.

MACHINE MECHANICS

Before Time:

Mechanic: This time machine is going nowhere. When it got smashed up, it smashed the hard drive. It's finished.

Time traveller: That is bad, so I shall have to go away and think about what I am going to do. You can keep the scrap, maybe use them for spare parts.

Sometime later, three lifetimes later (one lifetime is twenty years), I have it. I shall make myself road legal. I got my license updated from a paper license to a plastic photo license.

Part #1: Motorbike compulsory bike training (CBT)

Part #2: Motorbike theory test

Part #3: Motorbike 125 test pass

Part #4: Motorbike any size test pass

Part #5: Car (automatic) lessons

Part #6: Car theory test

Part #7: Car (automatic) test pass

Further Time:

In a life before now, I am fighting on the eastern front against the Nazi military machine with one shot of vodka before each battle. We fought army after army until we broke through.

The only thing is no one told us when to stop, so when we reached the beautiful emerald isle that is Britain, I didn't realise it would be full of foreigners.

No time—Let me in.

Then a voice says, Go away.

Okay, if you don't want to know.

The door opens. What is it? And don't shout—I feel dead to the world.

One hour later, you have spent a whole hour talking a load of gibberish. Just go away. See you whenever. The door slams.

My head feels like it is all over the place.

P.S., I fixed time. First, I need a shell. Bang, crunch, sort, found, done. Got my remedy sorted. Now for the cogunatives. Must ensure left to right, right to left, wrong to right, left to left, right to right. Now for the energy source. I must remember the quantities and thrust amounts. Delicately does it, and then the future awaits.

> F. T. Note: The parts are transparent, but in my
> memory, the intelligence is correct. They do fit.

THE ILENTRISICAL TIMELINE

What I am about to say is what I saw and thought. I will explain it once I have said it!

I decide to take a journey in the Orbital because I want to see the world after the COVID-19 pandemic.

I set the solaric to five years after the fact. When I emerge from the Orbital, I am at the edge of a wood, and I walk to a green field. I look to the housing estate in the distance, where I lived in the 1960s, and the ground I am on now is a housing estate. I look at my watch; it is 10:15 p.m. Something in my mind tells me I am offsetting for some reason. I walk stealthily towards the housing estate; it is a drab evening. I walk over to the courtyard and to the house I lived in. There are no lights on, so I walk through the wall and into the main living room. I take a seat and pick up a newspaper lying nearby. The headline reads, 'Nuclear War Has Begun.

I start to crack up, and as I crumple the newspaper, I am overwhelmed with tears. I hear movement, so after putting down the newspaper, I walk through the wall of the front of the house and cross the small garden, the path and road, and then the fence of a school. I lean on the fence, still crying. Upon realising a molten-hot sensation, I see my hands go through the iron railings.

I walk and think to myself, *I can and must stop this. Is this why I failed my career? Is this why my expectations disappointed me? Is this why the trash bin was overflowing?*

Then I stop in my tracks and think, *Am I being misled by the Orbital because it has already happened? Did the Orbital use safety protocol?* I turn around and walk back to the Orbital, realising I didn't see anyone. I open the door and close it once inside. I then set the coordinates and am gone.

F. T. Note: Career: Korea War

        Expectations: Vietnam War

        Trash Bin: Gulf War

START TO FINISH

As I got out of the Orbital, I walked into the thick darkness of the wood and stood on the edge. I looked out onto the green sway of grassland and waited. Then before my eyes, deep below in the grassland, the most ferocious predator of the prehistoric era walked by.

When I was sure it had passed, I moved out of the dark, thick wood and into the light.

I then entered the Orbital and set the solaric to lift up, ready for a transfix departure. While watching the view below on the monitor, I passed the Tyrannosaurus as I head towards space. The vision of the creature was bad, but it acted as if it knows something is moving in the sky.

I am on the edge of time. Everything is a silhouette of colours and shapes. I know it is the edge of time because everything is dissolving, creating the sensation of nothingness. I know I am reading my end, so I try a transfix, 'As if the parts around me, I know them'. I think of the sum of the parts, and it is as if realisation appears around me. Then as the surroundings of the Orbital become realisation to me, I start thinking, *I hope I didn't destroy anything*. Then a wondrous light show goes shooting past me.

My memories of making the Orbital are of being at the core of the universe. Then with each part required, I would go away and retrieve it. How it was there, I don't know, but it was. I do know it took me thirty-four years and seven and a half hours to make.

My understanding of how I did it is, as I registered, what I wanted to do with my matriculation of spare time. My mind did transfix on the necessary parts and requirements for said parts. Then I knew how to fix said parts together and in which order. It was truly a moment I treasured when she started up.

F. T. Note: I have been back to the core, and the sum of the parts does equal the time taken to create.

ARUA #1

It is the year 7543, and I am on the outer limits of known space. I have been living on Arua for exactly one year. It is a poisonous planet that has caught many an unsuspecting spaceship off guard. They think it a cloud of dust and have tried to travel through it, and because of its toxicity, the poisonous aura has eaten the unsuspecting travellers alive, leaving no trace that they were ever there. Truly a deadly planet. Beacons have been set up by caring explorers to warn passing spaceships of the imminent danger if they were to enter the planet's atmosphere.

With the invention of Silotine, a fibrous element, it has been possible to live on the planet, but not to venture outside.

The material was discovered in 5692. People are able to move about by teleportation. The house cost me 75,000 egots, or about 75 million pounds.

It's nice. You have neighbours two hundred to four hundred miles away. It's possible to visit by teleport.

I have just finished taking apart the Orbital. Not that I thought there was anything wrong, but I wanted to see it in all its glory.

I am looking at it strewn all over the basement, about fifteen thousand pieces. It looks glorious. There are Tennz fixings, panels, triggers, and buttons. The solaric is in bits, as are the fibre screen, dios, seats, abourize, three Tricons, and other parts.

I can't wait to get started to put it together.

ARUA #2

There is a space station that acts as a market—out in space of course. It is where spaceships arrive and dock for supplies, as well as to rejuvenate their fuel tanks. It is a good place; all products are sold at a fair price because if they weren't, people would simply rob them. Nonetheless, security is tight because they are on the outskirts of known space. Every three or four months, gigantic tankers roll up to replenish the station and help weary space travellers get supplies and desperately needed spares for their ships if they are not available on the station.

Anyway, it is a great place to go if you want to know what is happening in known space. The news is not good. I am sad to say the big powers, the Confederation of Planets and the Federation of Planets, are threatening each other, so people are saying war is imminent. Both are vying for support from independent and other planet unions. It seems the outlying planets are still as independent, and it is costly if you are not armed to the teeth, as they have always been.

ARUA #3

Well, I have just tried to buy some Abourize, but no one seems to know what it is, so it is a wasted journey. Just the usual supplies of food, drink, and reading material, and then I will head home.

After putting the Orbital back together and polishing it, I make sure all is shipshape. This has been emotional. The Abourize I have is still good enough to energise the Orbital. I think I was simply fooling myself that leaving a legacy in known space would work.

After making sure that the residence looks clean. I board the Orbital and put in the coordinates of a parking space on the station.

I give my 49 remaining egots to a family of three who were set upon and robbed. I also give the keypad and sign over the residency to them. I then say a few farewells, slip away, and set the coordinates on the Orbital.

FINAL FRONTIER

I am sitting inside the Orbital and have decided to have one last adventure on the far side of known space. I set the coordinates for Earth, and I set the time for the beginning of the end of the Roman Empire in Britain.

I arrive just outside of a place called Winchester. It looks rich, and I imagine things will get more rugged the farther north I go. I don't mind saying I look well set to go armed to the teeth with a shield, a couple of daggers, and a sword. I travel by night to avoid enemies on the road.

I arrive in a place called Stafford and stop at a tavern. While drinking and eating, I am approached by a young man, a thief. We start talking, and I buy him a keg and pie. Then after returning from somewhere, he tries to cut my purse. As if in slow motion, I say, 'if you touch, I will chop your hand off, so sit down.' Then I explain to him, 'If you ride with me, I will answer your deepest desire.'

He agrees and tells me he wants to be a king amongst greatness. Then after a rest until the coming of evening, we set off.

Just outside Birmingham, we meet a person begging, and I say to him, 'Why do you beg from their kind?'

He says, 'Because they just take from me.'

I explain to him, 'Then don't come with us, and I will give you your deepest desire.' He agrees and tells me he wants to know honour amongst others. I then obtain two horses so we can all ride, and we spend the rest of our time fitting out for the journey.

As I expected, the land gets rugged the father north we go. Just outside Newcastle, I meet a giant of a man. When he comes across to the stream, we are watering our horses. I say, 'Heading north?'

He replies, 'Yes, if that is the way you are going.'

I say, 'Come with us, and I will give you what you hope for deep inside.'

He says okay and says he wants to be the leader of a vast army.

We head onwards, travelling only at night. We skirt Hadrian's Wall, a so-called defence by way of mud swamp, safe from prying eyes.

FINAL FRONTIER #2

This is where things got dangerous. I wanted an army, so we spent the next few nights collecting volunteers from south of the border. I got near one hundred. Our armament looked like a joke. I took thirty volunteers, and we skirted the south wall and found one of their armouries. After gutting about a dozen Romans, we emptied the place of all food (bread, grain, and cheese) and ransacked the armoury (swords, spears, bows and arrows). Bryant, Darkness, and I covered our rear while Advant led at the front. It took us until almost dusk to complete the mission.

Before carrying on, I paid the shadows seven gold coins. They wanted ten to let us keep our food and weapons.

Once into the central highlands, I explained our mission. The only place possible for fortification was up north, so that was where we made camp. It was cold and rugged but was good for our purposes.

Advant took charge of the cooking, weapons, and supplies. Bryant took charge of military training skills. Darkness was the eyes in the back of my head. If he thought I missed something or something was wrong, he pushed us to keep the others on their guard. We made our own weapons along with the plunder and soon looked like a force to be reckoned with.

We made several monthly journeys for recruits and were around 1,500 strong when the call to arms came. With all our planning, which I never did without the others' backing, we converged on the centre highland for the big push.

Before leaving and talking with the others, we ordained Darkness as our king.

FINAL FRONTIER #3

There are over one hundred thousand of us at the gathering. Queen Boadicea's camp is at the centre, and the message comes that the leaders are sequestered to attend a war council. The next day, Darkness and I attend, and it is decided that the best of the knowledge stays with the Queen, so Darkness explains our overwhelming necessity to the mission, and I return to the clan or outlanders. When our purpose is confirmed by message, I am well pleased as I explain to Advant and Bryant our purpose.

As the first obstacle, Hadrian's Wall is overwhelmed with little trouble because of plummeting protection deficits. It is unceremonially pulled apart. Then while sweeping down the west coast, we burn and kill anything and anybody connected to the Romans. Bryant is leading the army, and two hundred of us are protecting the Peace Corps and wiping out any leftovers. Once we join up with the twenty-five thousand strong force of the Welsh camp, an aura of the whole island burning is all that exists.

We are told to wait at the border of Cornwall for Boadicea, for the final push. A few days later, we sweep through Cornwall but must watch the ships escape, carrying our welcome to them on our island.

The army of the Welsh forces is left to plunder and burn the west coast while we sweep eastwards. While passing near London, my wrist time switches on, and I am standing outside the Orbital. With remorse, sadness, and happiness, I climb inside and depart to a new destination.

P.S., I got my attire, a gold coin, and a horse by robbing some Romans.

F. T. Note: It was on this quest that I stopped and checked out the definitives of the Orbital.

LOST AND FOUND

It has been fifty years since I left known space. I know this because I set the solaric to awaken me if, in the allotted time, no existence of life was found.

Being in a special contortion, I have decided to take this chance to activate a resistal activation. A spatial contortion is when something looks bigger on the inside than on the outside. I have placed a resistor in an activation tube and connected it to an outside source on the solaric. It's only a temporary setup, until the molecular structure is stable enough to be solution activated into a Dyonise crystal, which will make it strong enough to maintain its own energy source.

First I gave everything a good wipe-down so no negative agitation might be intercepted. Then I switched on the solaric drive to maintain an independent energy source. I put on a breathing helmet. After setting the solaric to close, I stepped outside. I look around and am amazed at the sheer emptiness. I start going through different calculations on my wristband. Twenty minutes later, I open the door and step back inside. After a few moments of getting adjusted, I think to myself, *A job well done.*

I put the helmet and wristband in the utility cupboard and sit down. Then I set the solaric to carry on with the voyage and press the button, feeling very pleased with my up-and-coming world.

REAL THING

It's been fourteen years since the end of life incantation started shooting past my time machine. I watch the remnants of the silhouette passing into the distance. I have now decided to carry on with my journey. I enter the Orbital, set the solaric for signs of life, and press on.

To pass the time, I decide to write a story about time travel and motion.

'When in a prehistoric cave, I came upon a cave painting. A twig-like man, and a spear flying towards a bull-like creature.' Then after looking at the painting of the spear, I throw my mind, and it was like watching the spear travel through time, having adventure and bringing honour to the tribe it fought for!

It's been two months before I get a read on a sign of existence. It's what I have been searching for, so I set the coordinates and go towards it. I stop the Orbital just outside the atmosphere, which looks like three gases intertwined. My intentions are to investigate what I have found.

F. T. Note: What wonders or dangers have I come upon?

PLANET OF WONDER

I am standing outside of the Orbital. I have just sent in an oddball, a ball-shaped object to give me a readout of the various gaseous surroundings surrounding the planet.

The oddball soon returns, and I read it.

The atmosphere is made of three things:
>Sodime, which shuts down the regulatory system.
>Odium, which decimates particle parts.
>Trizine, which liquidates bits.

Conclusion: I can't wait to get to the surface of the planet. I am preparing to time travel to the planet's surface.

I have been on the planet for three years, and it is as amazing as I hoped it would be. There are plants that, when you sniff them, they gulp you whole and, when finished, spit you out. There are invisible, flying insects that fly through solids. There are colourful giant beasts that seem to be fruit eaters. There are many different fruits which seem to give out different hallucinogenic sensations.

The planet itself is full of colour, and the lakes are a silver colour. The water is full of beautiful creatures. The seasons are weather fronts that last three to six months.

I decide to create a Dyonise crystal, so I have extracted the enclosed resistor and connected it to a genome drip. The genome is made of parts and conforms to the readout of the Orbital.

It has been suspended in antigravity because the genome drip keeps getting hotter with each drop. What a wonderful site as the resistor disintegrates, and as the particles fall, they join together again as a Dyonise crystal.

I then put the crystal in the activation tube and connect it firmly. With its own energy back in the Orbital, I decide it is now time to search out other worlds.

PLANET HOLUVENA

I am in the Orbital, above a planet. I have been observing it for a while. It looks like a strange, dark, and morbid place. The strangest thing is it is a dark and dusty place on the surface, and there are lots of caves and holes that run deep inside the mass of the planet. After switching off the demigraph, I decide to go to the surface of the planet and explore. I teleport to the surface with enough supplies for twelve days, and I can't wait to see what the plant is beholden to.

I have been walking for six days now, and the surface of the cave system is all the same just jagged rock, with a dusty rock walk surface. The only light I have to see my way is a headlamp and a torch. It's like a labyrinth, weaving this way and that, except there is more than one exit.

I stop to rest and take off my backpack. First, I take out my zoom heater; that and my insulated flight suit makes it ideal. I am fine for visibility, so I take out a vitamin pill, which I have been doing every evening for a food supplement. I reflect on my journey so far. The structure has not changed. The temperature is constant at six degrees Celsius.

I am eight days into my journey when I come upon a wonderful site: an oasis of plant growth on a small island surrounded by water. The temperature has shot up to twenty degrees Celsius. The ceiling seems to be a cluster of many different coloured crystals, which probably creates the light effect.

There are large plants with green and purple petals and others with red and yellow flower heads. The grass is about four feet tall, and the trees are of medium height. The water is a pure, deep blue.

PLANET HOLUVENA #2

I take a sample of the water. After I place the stopper back on the tube, I hear a rumbling sound, which I instantly recognise as destruction. I pick up my pack and start running the way I came. In my haste, I drop the tube, and it breaks. I get a small container out of my backpack, put the two parts of the tube in it, and then place it in my pack.

I look in the direction of the devastating sound and realise it is getting closer. I check my wristband and enhance the tracking of the way I came from. Then I evolve the signal to teleport out of the labyrinth and onto the planet surface. Once on the surface, I put on my helmet and then teleport to the Orbital. Once inside, I quickly place a readout on the solaric, off eastbound, and press the button.

I switch on the demigraph and watch as the planet explodes into disintegrating particles. I then realise it was not the birth of a planet or the growing of a planet which I found—it was a planet preparing to go supernova. It seems life on the planet had eaten the planet so much that it could not sustain it anymore, so the planet ate itself to the point of self-destruction.

As the Orbital speeds away from the supernova aftermath, I take the canister from my pack. Using a mini soldering iron and a round metal oval, I shape the melted glass into the shape of the planet and put a sparkling coloured piece off-centre to represent the oasis. As for the stopper, I meld it into a shape for the model to sit on.

F. T. Note: The particles are like friends saying farewell to each other. The aftershock is like tears of goodbye.

TIME EXPANSE

The time machine has exploded, and now we are hurtling towards wherever. There are eight of us going in the same direction. One after the other, one of us extends our velocity, leaving the rest of us in its wake, until I am left alone.

It seems like an eternity before I see any form of anything. The expanse is all the time looking the same, endless and full of emptiness.

I pass weirdo Zeus reading a parchment with a sense it is looking down at me out of the corner of its eye. I pass a group of nature storms having like a conference about what to do next.

Then I slow down, and in a feeling of slow motion, pass a group of planets. I miss the smallest by what felt like a hair's breadth but was really thousands of miles.

I keep moving, and then I hit Earth's gravity, which shakes me. After picking up speed, I hurtle towards the planet's surface, and I am there.

I am in the middle of a bacterial war and see a window closing. I continue fighting knowing that victory awaits.

After fighting to the death looking for the missing link, I see it, but it turns the other way, so I miss. Then a feeling of 'I am not there' comes over me, and as I sink, I watch the Omo head towards the surface to join the others.

DIE TO LIVE

Polio: I am sorrow. My body doesn't want me; it has closed its heart to me.

Leprosy: You look at me in disdain. I look at me in disdain, so why am I here?

Cholera: Leave me here in the gutter to wash away so I can rise another day.

Smallpox: What I am, what I see, nobody understands me. I have to leave this place.

Typhoid: I'm so cold. Where am I? Where's my head at? Let me out of here.

Leukaemia: In my heart, I know I'm here, but I am there. Slowly I feel I shall fall apart, knowing in myself I shall part.

Pneumonia: I am so cold. I know when I close my eyes, I shall be no more.

Agony: I am in so much pain. When it goes away, I know it shall return because I am possessed.

Coronavirus: I shall stand and fall over and over. My fate is sealed.

Death: Don't be sad, don't be mad. You never knew me. I never wanted to be part of a world that didn't want me.

F. T. Note: You cannot add memories of the past with the future when you die when there are different life scenarios. So calculate what you know to expand belief into a memory.

I HAVE WATCHED, I HAVE SEEN

Before you read this, think of the saying 'Without change, you die'.

The planet is evolving, starting with a quake the length of the Canada and US border. The temperature is −175°C and dropping. Suddenly, a mighty roar screams, 'Death to you all.' The borders divide, with Canada rising like a giant towards the sky. America splinters like it is no more, like the rising of Hawaii. What a firecracker display fit for the gods. Then four months later, visions of the remains are visible.

In the Atlantic, the tension of Britain is finally broken like a bomb. The pressure of the sea explodes, taking out London like a fireball. Like a great ship, it snaps in half and is no more.

Then in a dome of silence, Atalenz rises from the bottom of the ocean in the middle of the Atlantic.

As quick as the glasses rise in Erie like a ghost, a massive tidal wave sweeps over it, incarcerating the European frontier and forcing it to rise from the pressure without.

The force of division by the pressure collapses Eastern Europe as it evolves in and is swept away by the incoming sea.

North Africa and Asia Minor are pulverised by incalculable pressure and then crumble like bricks into nothingness from shockwaves of the rising of the island nation, which engulfs the Samoan isles also hitting the isles of Indonesia disintegrating them. What is left of India and China are dressings of the Himalayan mountain range. Japan and Australia rise as if they didn't exist in their former form. The oasis of magic is born.

Back in the western hemisphere, the shock causes the red mountains of the south to rise. Then places called Texas, Mexico, and the West Indies are devoured into non-existence as if by a great sea monster. A new continent in its own right is born.

The echo of South America is moaning, but at what cost? This was the creation of the Bay of Absence.

P.S., I have seen enough and so set the controls to the arranged coordinates and press the button for time and space.

PLANET END

I am trudging in darkness towards the Orbital to escape the planet. I reach the time machine, open the hatch, and climb in. I have never been happier to get away from a place.

All the time while walking there, I think, *What once was will soon be isn't.*

Inside, time is of the essence. I set the controls for the far reaches of north by northwest, at 57 degrees. My emotions suddenly grab me, so I spend time having a shower. But still my emotions have me in their grip.

I try to sleep. Afterwards, I check the speed stick, which is at full disperse, and the reading on the directional finder is correct. The silicoscope shows what I did not want to see. The planet is glowing like a tiny dot of red, green, and then blue.

I know I have to keep going in a straight direction, gaining as much distance as I can from whence I came. Because of the debris and atmosphere, if my ship is caught in it, the inward pressure would stop me like a piece of tin. Still sweating, I try for some more sleep.

The first thing I do when I awake is check the silicoscope and see what I wanted to see—that is, nothing.

A new dawn of experience has arrived. I get my act together, slow the speed, and check the surroundings. I look around, and everything seems as it was. I can't remember the last time I felt emotionally thankful.

It is as if an age has passed, and I sit down and start thinking. I had put the Orbital down on the planet at one of the worst points of decimation.

I had endangered myself and the Orbital, but I got through it. I simply couldn't let hope pass. The disintegration is slowly heading towards the Earth's core, where with a flickering heat surge, the fate of the planet would be sealed.

THE PLANET

I am looking at a planet through the silicoscope on board the Orbital. At the moment, it is using up all my sense of calmness because it is about to go supernova.

With devastating impetus, the planet cracks in half. One half travels towards the sun, where it will voyage until it ends up on the other side; it has induced enough energy to last, as if a newborn planet will rise and discover an acknowledged procurement in space.

The other half has evolved on a special vortex to travel around space with witty thinking and preservation of energy, to become and grow as a space pirate. It is preserving its existence by dealing with terrestrials as it passes their time expanse.

Here is where I am honoured to be able to witness. Where the planet's structure parted, the structures that crumbled off and are left have been evolving in a silent group. Now they are shooting off on various paths as if comets, meteors, or asteroids in the aura of the cosmic belt. To have witnessed a millennium of existence is fantastic and shows the importance of not interfering with the time continuum.

I think, *What caused a planet of such age and created wisdom to decide not to carry on? Was it a lack of energy? Go figure, and may saints preserve us. Or was it total negativity? That is of no use.*

P.S., It was the planet Ganitz, considered to be the oldest planet to have ever existed.

JOURNEY

I land the time machine and switch it down. I have travelled to the planet Mystique, where giant beasts roam. Their ferocity is matched only by their exuberant texture. For those who do not know, it is a mysterious place, and if you do not keep your mind focused, you can easily lose it.

The ecology of the planet is sustained from the ferocity of the variety of beasts that roam, as well as by the exceptional quality of the endeavour of the plant life. Whereas they use rays of fire, the plants use bounce. Like the beasts, they too are giants of wonderous sight. It is an ecology that is beholden to being as its surroundings.

I am heading towards a colony called Wizarz, which cannot be located on land or from space. It is a place protected by a dome of nothingness, where those who have magic powers have crossed through the void to the realm of their own kind.

I take the bracelet of existence from my utility belt and place it around my wrist. Instinctively I am drawn in the direction of the colony. As I reach the dome of naught, I sense its presence; it is as if it is the end of a late night, and I am in a different place. I walk over a big hill looking at how nice a place it is. From the top of the hill, I see the town, which looks simple and nice. Inside, I set up my stall with books, pictures, and bric-a-brac (an orb, a piece of iron) with the important sign 'Teller of Tall Stories'. After a heck of a day, I suddenly feel thirsty and hungry. I go for a walk, passing wooden shacks and all kinds of different outlandish buildings.

With a heart of joy and sorrow, I think I could stay here forever—which is my call to say I have been here a while, so it is now time to go. I check that I have no egots left and put the bracelet on my wrist. Then I put up a sign that says 'Apprentice Needed' and depart.

P.S., After giving the Orbital a good working over to let it know how much I love her, I secure the hatch and set the controls for empty space. I decide to visit a place that a pirate would call Treasure Planet.

VIEW

The universe is a fascinating place of different shapes and colours. It makes you want to observe because each particle you look at or each way you look upon it is different. Then there is the fact that it is beautiful to set your sights on.

You want to look and learn about it because there are so many mysterious and so faraway places. Different segments are given different names. Stars that seem to change their shape (twinkle) are thousands of miles away, if not millions. Sometimes they are looked upon as shooting stars, passing at speed through space. There are planets that are located throughout space. Sometimes they are alone with celestial bodies for company. At other times, there are groups of planets, which are known collectively as galaxies. There are also the suns which are thought to give off different forms of energy to help sustain life on other planets.

Then there is the cosmos, where a part of space is considered to be an area of emptiness. *Terrestrial* is a sight relating to seeing from the planet Earth. Sphere is a solid where all parts lead to a core part as its mainstay. A black hole is a powerful existence which pulls anything in using its gravitational pull.

Another phenomenon is the Milky Way, the galaxy that includes the Earth. There are also rainbows, asteroids, comets, meteorites. A supernova is when a planet explodes, creating a bright light. A solar system is a group of planets, moons, and other celestial bodies.

P.S., All of the above is known collectively as the universe.

It has been described differently in mythology, where the above is recognised as heaven or a destiny in the afterlife. Then there is hell, where very bad people go deep within the bowels of the planet in their afterlife.

The human race has slowly been trying to reach the extremities of space, by sending up satellites to observe, communicate, and map space. They also achieved a landing on the moon and created a space station in space. The human also walked in space.

The problem with this is the more they boast of fervour in space, the worse the problems are on planet Earth.

PLANET TRIZON

I have arrived at my special coordinates after a three-hundred-day sleep in suspended animation. I now want to clean myself up and go see what all the fuss is about.

I land the time machine and then explore the surroundings. The mountains are made from gold, and there is a platinum core and stream in the beauty of that pretence. This reminds me of something, so I get some sunglasses to protect my eyes. I then come upon the Diamond Sea and its diamond shimmers.

I spend the next three days living under the stars and enjoying the richness of the planet's good sustenance. I go for a swim in the mystical Diamond Sea and see the beautiful serpent fish swim between the different cuts of temperament, depending on which is their refinement. I head for the colony of Blinz, and when I get there, I have a fabulous three days. Then I get a strange visit from an envoy, who requests I talk to the goron at the grand chamber. I accept, and the following day, I visit the goron, Chabiv. After we say our hellos, he asks me if I will check out some Confederation vessels that have been scanning their border. It seems that it is unusual, and they want to know if they should prepare for war. I think it over and decide it is okay. For the next two days, I journey back to the time machine. I enter the Orbital and make a plan for the clandestine operation.

I am orbiting planet Trizon in stealth mode, with all incoming scopes for a thousand miles closed down. Then I catch a reading of a Confederation vessel. I set the contact strands for an area readout. I then set the mode for a torrential downpour. The directional finder goes towards the Confederation vessel.

When I start splicing through the vessel, I catch glimpses of the deck crew. I closely check that the download has gone from red (stand by) to blue (activated) and then green (complete). Once through, I enable a constant stealth speed, ensuring there is no jump on the wavelength monitor.

Once I am sure the vessel is moving away from me, I stay in stealth mode and set my coordinates for the planet. Once I am orbiting the planet, I telegraph the goron and have an emissary meet me outside the city. I teleport down and give the chip to the envoy.

A strange thing, dealing with espionage. Don't get me wrong—I have great respect for outliers.

TIME WATCH

- I am a time traveller. Really, it is just that my watch has stopped.
- I walk through stone; my mind has purpose. I walk through a wall; there is nothing there. I wait at the bottom of the sea, I look inside the chest it is empty. I wait no more.
- If there is no time, then what time is it? Yay, got that dead to rights!
- Blasted time, forgotten time. Rotten time, no time.
- I knew there was something I forgot, and that is: I forgot to set the time!
- Why go into hypersleep and be woken in time! Why not think a thought and awaken then? Don't forget purpose. Save a lot of time wasting.
- Being banished for all time will create a space distortion, which will create a space rivet with an explosion of magnitude where existence is not wanted. Antimatter will not tolerate what is not theirs.
- As I forge through time, I am envisioned. When I get mixed up, I lose time.
- When it's time, I will be ready.
- Comment? For what?
- Answer: For the future—what else?

TIME EMERGENCE

- Time waits, time creates, time gives you more.
- All the time in the world, just a waste of time.
- I gave up my time for you, and you took all that time.
- From the beginning of time to the end of time.
- I cannot remember the first time I saw you because it went into the future. But I can remember the last because time stopped.
- If time stops, would you think of it? No, because you would be lost in time.
- Time is of the essence. Why is it important? Because a life depends on it.
- You don't change time; you simply change what is in it.
- The first time, the last time, once upon a time.
- You can create what is with you for all time. You can create that which is with you for a long time, and you can create that which is lost in time. (In an instant, that which is a void).
- When time ran out, it did not exist.
- Time is not everything; the burden is on you.
- While I wait in time, I lose time, but if it happens in time, I gain time.
- What is what when I lose time? It is but a figment of my imagination.
- For the last time, and I will not tell you again.
- Does that mean there is hope for the future?
- When was the last time you imagined that, whatever that was?
- Throughout time, humanity has built great cities and institutions to admire their creativity and created various forms of transport. Then to stop time, humanity has destroyed what it created.

- Time is not a dominant factor; it is just a sign of one's endeavour. Humanity would still go on without its creation.
- In time, I will get it together, meaning there is hope even when there is no time.

P.S., A question in time. Throughout time, humanity has shown fortitude to endeavour in tasks. Does that mean when time stops, so does human endeavour? Answered in time.

F. T. Note: A long time ago before time existed, there were dinosaurs. Lost in time were beasts, creatures, and serpents. If you should meet, say hello for me and see if you can get the time.

TIME MACHINE

Throughout history, a few wise and farsighted people have had the knowledge to succeed into the extradimensional movement of time travel.

One of the most famous, if not the most famous is Doctor Who, where, in the late 1950s, he created out of an emergency call box his time machine. His time travel process was to exasperate the solar stream, thus setting the mechanics to wherever he wanted to proceed. He was an old man when he completed his fantastic machine. As a young boy, he was sodomised as a monstrosity of birth because when he was born, he had two hearts.

When he took to his time travel adventure, he had a slight accident, and out in the far realms of space, he discovered that when he died, he could reincarnate and start a new life as another self-being.

It just goes to show that everything is not always as it seems.

The time tunnel, a lesser-known experience of time travel, was created in the 1960s by a group of scientists working for the American military. A time travel–obsessed scientist, Tony Newman, sought to prove his theory and created the going concern. To try to bring him back, they brought in another scientist named Doug Phillips, thus creating uncontrolled time travel.

They were successful in both returning, but because of various actions in their travels of interfering with the time continuum, their return caused a fusion of nuclear capacity, which caused an explosion, destroying all evidence of its capability.

In 1932, George Wells of University London created a time machine which used the capabilities of clock time enhanced by a quart of plutonium. The time clock on the machine moved forward or backwards, whichever way the time control lever was pulled. The capabilities were limited to the surroundings changing in time. The time machine itself did not move unless moved physically. The travel experience was stopped by centring the lever.

A lessor known time traveller, John Almond, created his time machine on the enactment and transparency of alchemy, meaning an astronomical breakdown to the equivalent compounds.

Mine is built on time warp control capacity that splits space at a given point, meaning from once was to once is. If you're wondering about the eternal bracelet, it is a mini Orbital that, when you add devotion, calculates time and encompasses it.

P.S., Dr Who, may the waves lift you up and send you forth before and beyond.

F. T. Note: Saints preserve us. May our paths never cross.

MINE TO THROW

While blasting through time, all you can see is the devotion and caring for that moment of what you do. Caught in time, all you sense is the insignia of defeat creeping up on you and the sense of panic. The question is, Can I get out of it, and if I do, will I regret missing out (meaning being taken in and stupid to the fact)? That is a problem. You are not a changeling and can't comprehend what to do. That is probably why a time traveller is through with the consequences before it acts on them. That is why when it talks to you, sometimes you do not understand—because it is talking to you to the end of said sequence. A time traveller does not pass; it is simply lost in its machine of time.

When people speak to a time traveller, they are just their bragging or moaning about their situation because in the end, what they said is of no use and makes no sense. The legacy is all theirs because it is.

A moment in time when a time traveller stops is just a void or a directional finder of where a gateway might be. The question is, Are you capable of finding what you search for or want to obtain? And what do you do once you have found it? Also, have you the time for it?

A distance perspective of a time traveller has no meaning; it just throws its mind and flatlines at the same time. Then what it was simply once was. That is a bad omen for is, when a brainwave wants to know it all. All you want to do now is toddle off like a good boy. A self-indulging pleasure is that it is not possible, and then eventually it is so real for you.

As the tears fall, there are so many wonders to see and give a condition of ecstasy. So wonder no more. Travelling through mortal pleasures is an exquisite learning curve. Then while speeding up, it becomes a blur, but the joy and excitement live on. It gave me strength to forge on.

So far gone now, what you comprehend, and then time tells me what it reckons.

P.S., I have been waiting such a long time. Thank you so very much for that.

Where has everybody gone!

P.S.S., I have been waiting so long for you, I could write a book on it.

F. T. Note: You have to understand it is never that easy. Besides, what if it was not for you, meaning you paid for its ticket? What is all the fuss about?

EYE TO EYE

While sitting around a warm fire in the desert, under a red sun, I am watching stars appear and disappear in the sky. Then after looking in the distance, I spy a massive sandstorm coming towards me. I have decided I don't want to remain on the planet anymore, so I set the directional finder on the time machine to 'lasting evolvement' and then step outside to watch the arrival of the storm.

The time machine does not leave. I move towards the time machine, step inside, and ask the readout, 'Why?'

It reads, 'I am not leaving without you, I shall endeavour to take you home.'

DIALOGUES

Warning: These theses have not been recognised by any medical body or organisation.

GERM WARFARE

Germ Warfare #1

My first understanding of germs was back in approximately 1963, when different types of diseases were devastating countries around the world. Then after looking at the stars, I realised this nation of ours was a guiding light for airborne microorganisms to the new world.

So using the power of the stars, I started my own little war. With one infection after another, I ate it, and I won.

I feel so sorry that my little game did not cloak all of the nation.

My second encounter is from a memory I have of a Chinese man begging me for the antidote until finally I said, 'Say please,' and gave it to him. Before he departed, I said, 'Will I get it back?'

He said, 'Yes, I promise.'

As the door closed behind him, I thought, *Yes, says you and thirteen billion other Chinese.*

Note: Fact or fiction?

GERM WARFARE #2

In my study of the death stars, this is what I discovered.

- Polio: The dense sensation is a feeling of deprivation. All I could think was for nobody to touch me, or I would bust into bits. I could sense my body mechanism running on empty. After three days of anxiety and trepidation, I came out of it feeling as if I had been working hard all day.
- Pneumonia: The sensation of feeling so cold. I could not stop it, and I could not make sense of my surroundings. I can remember waking up with an icicle on my nose. When it was over three days later, I felt very weak.
- Malaria: Really strange, with feeling fine and then sweating being a recurring factor. When it was over three days later, I felt like I spent all day waking up.
- Cholera: I lay in bed feeling like I was on fire, and the intensity of the heat kept going up. I could not stop tossing about. When it was over, I felt empty inside.
- Coronavirus: A sensation as if your body is closing down on you. When you awaken, you feel lousy. Then it starts again, and with each occurrence, it feels worse than before. When it was over, I felt as if I had lots of energy to burn.

Note: Upon looking up to where the cluster of stars were and seeing an empty space, I thought I knew nothing I wanted anyone to learn about.

GERM WARFARE #3

I have left these notes out because of the strange expectation.

Smallpox, plague, Ebola—these are basically the same thing with similar symptoms, and they spread throughout communities, killing millions.

In my contact, it was like a wave closed down the organ systems of the body. The blood had deep bluish blotches where the bacteria pathogens had clogged up the flow. This caused the skin to turn whitish, with a non-breathable sensation. The eyes felt like areas of burning and welling water. The only part of the body that felt like it was still functional was the stomach, which contains hydrochloric acid which kills pathogens. For some reason, I felt I was living there. It seemed an age while moving towards the small intestine; it looked nice. Then, moving like a submariner after a short while, very cautiously I moved through the blood. When I reached the brain, I felt this was it and dissolved into nothingness.

When I awoke, I felt cold and weary. I had a feeling I wanted to thank someone.

Note: I had sorted out my deathly birth and was happy about it.

DEADLY INCANTATION

Leukaemia reminds me of life losses. It starts with a slight skin rash, then poxy lumps. At this point, the bod goes cold. Then blotches form in groups.

The eyes begin to decelerate; only the itching and strange body feeling (tiredness) keeps you awake.

While you are thinking of this, the small pimples, the lumps and red blotches, are spreading all over the body. By the end of a month, your whole body is a mass of pimples, lumps, and blotches, and their numbers keep increasing.

In the cloud, when they attack, they look just like nerve cells. Then damaging it looks like a hot air geyser. That is where I reckon all the putrid is forming from.

The formula for the cure is found in the Yakuza plant. You squeeze the bud, and a dark green liquid oozes out. While resting near dead, you mix the liquid in two parts water to one small container of liquid. (When there is no time, you gulp the liquid pure.)

After brushing past the immune antigen, you get a sense of it saying, 'I haven't finished yet.' Over the next few months or years, the red particles come and go. Then they start grouping again, and your mouth gets very sore as a memorandum sets in. You know you have fewer than four days to live, so you go to the only place that has the serum. You're all over the place every second, and it feels like an age.

In the distance, you see the hospital, with nothing but wasteland around it. It feels like you stumble and walk forever. You walk into the doctor's office. There, on the top shelf in the cabinet, is the cure labelled 'Leukaemia: mix two with one'.

I am exact, so I fill a bowl with two parts water and one part serum. Then lifting the bowl, I swallow the contents. I crawled home, and slowly my health returned. I have not seen the pimples, lumps, red blotches, or symptoms since.

During this secondary attack, you might end up with a large puss ball that keeps coming and going. Just get a pin, prick it, and squeeze the life out of it.

Note: Last memory of that place: one photo in the newspaper showed it standing eerily in the wasteland, and the photo next to it showed it as rubble after it got blown up in the wasteland.

WAR AGAINST THE WARMONGER

1. To the people who think taking disinfectants by injection or swallowing is wrong because it kills everything: the clear slime which you burp up after swallowing disinfectant is the air you breathe.

2. Whoever suggested hoarding people into groups to choose who should die and who should survive has a twisted sense of healthcare.

3. The person who thought of creating a particle fusion passport, putting a time limit on how long a person can be immune against diseases, is out of their skull. Diseases would go to town on that rubbish.

In the cloud, I did not go back in against COVID-19 to kill a sleeper for my health. I went back in to show the power of the immune system. After destroying the strain, the antitoxin didn't join the white blood cell train until my body was clear.

If it had gone wrong, I could have woken up paralysed, blind, or dead, and I did not nuke twenty-five million people for my health. I did it for the survivors of the Great War and their offspring. (That last part seemed important to add.)

Note: People say the strangest things sometimes.

CONSPIRACY THEORY

The headlines:

It has been three nerve-shattering years since the deadly attack by COVID-19 on the planet.

Despite the promises and hearsay by politicians, doctors and scientists are still nowhere in sight of the cure.

There are more than one million dead and seven and a half million injured rioters, mass murderers, and plague carriers in many countries.

With the discovery of child deaths related to coronavirus four months into the fight against it, my worst fears are confirmed: scientists do not recognise how dangerous it is.

The antigens are recognising the human organs' growth and rocketing through the human race.

Hope Incorporated has sent out an appeal for any facts or thoughts you may have on the virus. I promise you they will be investigated.

Note: Don't give up. Believe in hope like it believes in you.

THE SCIENTIST

The scientist slams open the door to his laboratory and runs over to the control room. While waving his sheets of paper, he shouts, 'Stop the satellite launch! You cannot launch yet! It is too soon! It's not clear.'

The man in the military uniform says, 'Don't be silly. I have read the findings, and they look good to me.' He looks at the military police security and says, 'Lead the scientist back to his laboratory.'

Surrounded by three security guards, the scientist is led across the dusty courtyard to his laboratory, mumbling, 'They have to stop. It's not right. It isn't clear.'

Three years later, in his laboratory somewhere in a secluded area, he looks up from his microscope and suddenly starts smashing everything and wiping everything from the counters. He then gets a can of gasoline from the boot of his car and pours it over the laboratory until it is empty. Then he drops the container and goes to his computer.

He sends three e-mails to three different scientists. Then he flicks the lighter and drops the flame on the gasoline. After making sure the blaze is engulfing the whole building, he gets in his car and drives to a clifftop. He revs the engine and releases the brake, sending himself to his death.

Note: The three e-mails all read the same: 'Do you cry in your sleep and wake up crying like I do? Because it was a failure, or because of what you did?'

CORONAVIRUS

Wake-up call: There will be no vaccine for COVID-19. Because of its devastating power as a weapon, the war machine will not stop at any cost to get its hands on it. It does not matter how long it takes to synthesise the cure; they will take and try to manipulate the properties. Like the atomic bomb, they want to create mass destruction first.

Genome + DNA = Manipulate.

Newsflash: No human DNA carries the gene that can create that kind of weapon.

Genome + DNA = Factualise.

I cannot believe you would follow me to the end of my life cycle and destroy my world again.

You thieves should watch yourselves!

You don't need another Philadelphia incident, especially right now.

P.S., I would rather sit on a dead planet and think, *So they finally threw you off*, than think, *I told you so.*

THE CROSSOVER

It is the year 1919. I am in my laboratory and have discovered how to manipulate and stop the coronavirus wave. By splitting polonium and using radio waves, the intensity of the COVID-19 wave slowed, and then disintegration occurred. This stopped the virus and its contamination effort.

I have one ball of polonium left, and with science's new discovery of fusion, I am going to take it to the science centre along with all my papers and hope they will perfect it. Then I can get out of this place. I was at the science academy for over three hours, addressing their stern faces and questions. I was happy when I returned. I opened the door, and it looked like a bomb had hit it.

Everything was broken or ransacked.

While walking around and feeling the crackling of glass underfoot, I came upon a dead body. He had a blood splatter with a hole in the middle of it, so I figured he had been shot. I looked at the face and had no recollection of seeing him before. I had no intension of ever being discovered, so I got a few things together and left. I suppose I should have checked the body for identification, but the pieces of the jigsaw are more important than some stiff trying to rob me.

Note: What is, was! Is this how it is going to be for the human race?

MY COVID-19 THESIS

Protection

How to protect ourselves against the virus:

1. Wash your hands with soap and water; it kills the bacteria carrying the virus.

2. Stay at home; that is the best chance of avoiding the parasite.

3. If you must go outside to buy food and drink, be sure to keep a good distance from others. Don't help it to spread.

4. When going outside, be sure to wear a face mask. You never know who is transmitting the disease via cough or sneeze.

P.S., We are all at the bus stop waiting for that miracle cure, the vaccine.

PART 2

These facts may sound trivial but are still important.

When a person is infected with COVID-19, they will feel they are being bombarded with a series of attacks. After each attack, they will feel that their body has been drained of its energy.

That is why people with underlying illnesses are in the most danger of death.

After the devastating attack on the body, because the immune system has been fighting with the virus, you will feel very weak, but this should pass in a couple of weeks.

People with underlying illnesses should be watched closely for at least three weeks.

The remnants of the attack, when destroyed, are collected by all three parts of the internal immune system and diffused into the bloodstream, where it is transported to the kidneys. Then it is transferred to the bladder, where it is disposed of in a very long wee.

HISTORY MAKER

Let me take you back to when all that existed was bacterium in a swamp. Eventually, the first land creature crawled out of that swamp. Before that itty-bitty creature crawled out of the swamp, there was a great bacterial war.

In a final throw of the dice, the bad bacteria, which I believe was nitro–oxide, fought with the good bacteria, oxy-oxide. When the two bacterium parted, the bad bacteria had been fooled and sank in the swamp. The good bacteria rose up, grew, and gave the beginnings of life on Earth.

That is why the bad bacteria which has now escaped the swamp after thriving in the depths seeks out the good bacteria.

WHAT OF IT

The COVID-19 virus is a fibrous optative. This means it divides and joins with the divisions through respiration.

It cannot be killed by phagocytosis because of rapid expansion.

It cannot be killed by antibiotics because it moves and expands too quickly.

It cannot be killed by normal antitoxins because it drains the antitoxins energy so it becomes too weak to destroy it.

The way to destroy the virus is from within.

The antitoxin, when looked at under a microscope, looks like a normal round cell. When it recognises the virus, it forms into an arrow and enters the virus.

Once within, it shocks the virus and causes the pulsating reaction to spread out, disintegrating the virus and thus killing it.

MARBLES

Destroying COVID-19 is like a game of marbles. If you block a hole before an opponent, you win.

But if your opponent wins, you cannot unblock that hole.

If you have to hit your opponent's marbles to win and your opponent throws one marble a long distance, most of the time you will have to expend extra energy to get him. Remember that as your opponent draws you in.

That is why coming from afar, your immune system (antitoxin) would act like an arrow, piercing the defences and causing a pulsating effect.

PRACTICAL EXPERIENCE

In the cloud, COVID-19 is a very dangerous particle to play with.

COVID-19 = combustible oxidized volume infectious disease.

This experiment should be carried out only in a vacuum.

If you take 19, which is an unknown mass of oxygen, and apply a drop of COVID, you will see a mass approximately half the size of the average human body and twice as wide.

Then you apply serum F2, GH6, and C3, and you will see the virus disperse to atom form.

DEATH COUNT

There is one thing that we are all united about with the coronavirus pandemic, and that is it has caused grief and sorrow throughout the world.

Starting in China, within four months it spread around the world. First the Orient, then Asia, then Africa, then Europe, then North America, and finally Latin America.

Most nations acted very quickly in instituting the preventive measures. Other nations eventually did so once they realised the gravity of the situation. The logistics of the situation soon became a big problem for nations both rich and poor: Insuring the availability of food for all. The availability of protective clothing for everybody.

The availability of respiratory machines for the sick.

It soon became clear when countries started reporting hundreds of people were dying by the day, and one by one, nations started reporting death tallies of ten thousand plus. The situation was desperate

A major issue developing was the loss of life of frontline workers through getting the symptoms or dying of the virus. God be with them.

One glimmer of hope came in April 2020, with China making claims of halting the pandemic.

P.S., Scientists must find a vaccine—not today, not tomorrow, but yesterday.

ENVELOPE EFFECT

Many decades ago, while searching for an end-of-days scenario, I was confronted by the coronavirus (again) in the form of three clouds. I now think I understand what they meant. When brushing two clouds apart, there was another cloud behind it. Its size looked to be the size of the first two clouds added together. This is what I think they meant! I am going to call it the envelope effect.

When cloud A finished devastating the planet, cloud B started causing aftershocks. Cloud C is sitting above the mountains across the planet and at the North and South Poles.

It is not moving because of the low density. I believe when the air pressure from below reaches the C cloud, it will be enough energy to split the cloud onto North America. In South America, it is the same thing, with a slight fold over Panama and into Mexico.

The coronavirus cluster sitting over the South Pole, when it gains enough energy, will head straight towards the coasts of Erie and Britain.

The cluster over the North Pole will split and cross into Canada and Russia.

UPDATE

I know when the disease attacked the planet.

I know the economic hardship it has caused and the emotional grief.

I just don't know when the vaccine is going to save the human race.

P.S., I have never believed in the phase 'Anything is possible' more than I do now.

PAST PRETENCE

'If my intelligence is correct …'

In a place on Weatley Street in London (later changed to Wheatley Street) in 1903, a scientist named George Graham started an experiment to create polonium. He discovered that by applying pressure, he could calculate that at a certain point, the droplet of a pathogen stayed steady at a certain number, and when reapplied to the pathogen, the pathogen did dissolve.

At this discovery, the scientist was ecstatic. He then started applying another pathogen, then another, and each time the number remained constant. He then reapplied the droplet, and the pathogen dissolved.

The number where the pathogen stayed constant was always a negative number.

This was a great breakthrough, and up to the year 1913, many lives were saved.

But in 1913, with the readouts always being constant, the scientist for some reason decided he was going to break the polonium sphere and discover its core content.

What he didn't realise was that the core factor was COVID-19, and breaking the sphere unleashed the first instincts of a nuclear reaction.

No matter how he tried, he could not get a steady negative readout again.

People called him a fluke; others called him a miracle worker. Call him what you like, but he performed a great service to humanity.

LOADED GUN SCENARIO

The United States is going through an unprecedented pandemic of coronavirus. It is my opinion, that this is because of the country's wilful neglect of the necessary precautions to stem the tide of the virus.

With all the mass demonstrations and mass gatherings, this has caused a quickening of the antigens to adapt to the human organism. Another is the wilful neglect to use a mask, thus not giving protection against the disease.

From cluster bombs that hit the country without warning to grenades that created flare-ups of the disease, now massive numbers of people are catching the virus every day. Now all the people who are ill with the disease shall die like a nuclear warhead going off.

One terrible realisation of the virus quickening is that the virus is now attacking and affecting not only old people but also younger people.

Is this what the rest of the world has to look forward to when the protection barriers in the world break down?

A terrifying realisation came to me. I thought of all the diseases that have been incubating in this country for the past two hundred years. If a vaccine is not found for the virus, then the only way to stop it is to drop a nuclear bomb on the place it is spreading. Remember: destroy the core, and you destroy the virus.

You may think that's mad, but what if the infected reached one billion, and still there was no cure? Do you think a desperate world would not search for any chance of a vaccine?

COVID-19 PROPHECY

The Coronavirus is a microbial particle which evolves around the planet. As time has gone on, it has diffused into the life and times of the planet.

With the discovery that in less than one hundred years, this planet will not be able to sustain the population, drastic action has been needed.

The coronavirus exists in the atmosphere as wavelengths, each different to the area it is adapted for. Now, the next millennium has awoken a new generation of life. The COVID-19 particle reacted to the future of the next generations for one thousand years, seeing what the last millennium left it!

By bringing the future and past together and finding the present, I have envisioned a fantastic outlook for the future, and I hope that it is true.

P.S., My thoughts are of being welcomed into the digital world and living it, where the human body becomes a different life form, ileum is the nervous system, and COVID is the particles of the body form.

TORMENTED MIND

It has been eight months since the virus struck planet Earth. What torment the human mind is being put through by the coronavirus pandemic.

They tell us that masks are of no use. Now they are insisting we wear a mask on the streets and in shops.

They say that track and trace is all-important in stopping the spread of the virus. Now they say track and trace will be of no use if there is a second flare-up of the disease.

They say we can gather in groups and go on holiday. Then suddenly there is a flare-up of the disease, and holidays are stopped. Those caught in the flare-up must quarantine for fourteen days, then only ten days.

When it comes to a vaccine, there have been various products that have been said to help against the virus. Then a few days later, they say that information was wrong. The World Health Organization has said there may never be a cure for the virus.

The western hemisphere is in turmoil because of the virus. Brazil, a country that has fought every step of the way against the lockdown because of the virus, has almost one hundred thousand dead. The United States, which at first went with the rest of the world with lockdown and then quickly started resisting it, has over 150,000 dead. Now, many states are trying to reverse the consequences of opening the country too early.

The rest of the world is still trying to resist the virus. But Mexico and India, which are both very poor countries, have made statements that lockdown is near impossible. They are suffering and getting worse from the virus

P.S., The western hemisphere is so badly devastated by the coronavirus that this is where the virus plans to make its home on Earth.

NEXT WAVE

It is now eight months since the first attack of COVID-19. Now there has been a lull in the infection rate, but the world is waiting for a second wave.

Signs that the next wave of infection has begun include signals coming from South Korea, Sichuan Province, Hong Kong, China, and Australia.

The speeding up of the infection rate is being felt all around the world.

Nine months since the start of the pandemic, Europe is now beginning to feel the effect of the second wave, with Germany, Greece, and France reporting large numbers of new cases. Other countries in Europe are also reporting large outbreaks of the virus.

New Zealand has reported its first new cases of the virus in over one hundred days. The United Kingdom at this time is experiencing outbreaks in Blackburn, Leicester, Aberdeen, and more.

P.S., In the cloud, the alphabet is spelt in a jumble to discover the genome. A drop of COVID-19 is dropped into the start process, and the cure is the resulting factor F2, GH6, C3. I attempted this experiment twice, and the result was the same. The cure is a genome that can formulate the whole as a part.

ROLLING RIFT

It is nearly November 2020, and the coronavirus pandemic is exploding. The number of dead is over one million, and the number of infected is approaching fifty million.

With the number of people being affected, the virus is regenerating at an exponential rate, with no sign of it slowing down. As the might of the coronavirus surges onwards and upwards, I do not think it will be long before the rolling rift falls upon China from the northern hemisphere and from Brazil and onto America in the western hemisphere.

If my predictions are correct, this will occur around June 2021. Then the fusion of the two warring factions will create a positive effect, meaning the virus will become whole with a floating tolerance. This should nullify the armament effect.

Anything left with the number dying and the number infected must be put down to collateral damage as the phoenix spreads its wings.

P.S., Stay in there. I won't give up the fight like the madman who says no to a vaccine. I know somewhere inside, you care.

VIRUS SAVE

If for any reason my thesis for saving the human race is a fake, have a gander but hang on tight. It's scary. With the human race terrified and transfixed on something called a vaccine, the next stage is petrifying.

As the world turns and the virus speeds up and evolves, speeding up to the planet's velocity, it will succeed it and break off into space.

The problem with this is that it takes many lives with it because of the connection between living recognition and breathing the coronavirus.

P.S., Because of their sentiments there, life support should see them farther than any other into the realm of the above before their will gives out.

DIVULGENCE

Looking into the mind of a virus.

I am a bringer of death, a destroyer of worlds.

I am Corni; you are a WHO.

I live for you, and you die for me.

I have no time; you have told me so and keep telling me so. You and your oohs and aahs that you apply unto your kind, striving to die for no reason.

I am a race apart; your mind is in phooey land.

I am one, a destroyer of worlds.

As I suffer with the torment of a human life form and realise that there is but one end, I plan for and slip into the deliverance of death to divulge my form. As I stand upon the mushroom bomb, you look down a microscope, but I imagine me upon you.

P.S., As you look into the future and see a mirage of the changing anatomy of the human life form, I think that is probably why some of you are still alive.

FUSION

Since the coronavirus spread over the whole planet, it has been hitting with lethal force, starting with cluster bombs, then grenades and bullets, and finally with the lethal force of nuclear warheads.

People in the northern hemisphere are walking around with the strange sensation of walking inside a nuclear explosion. It is a strange sensation; it feels warm and safe.

The people of the western hemisphere are in a state of panic. They are only now realising that what they did has a 'no way back' ending. By not following lockdown protocol, if my prediction is correct, then between Christmas Day 2020 and New Year's Day 2021, the amalgamation of the virus attack will fuse together into a thought process of seek and kill.

P.S., Human war's footprint is just imagery.

DEPARTURE

It is now December 2020, and I feel the COVID-19 pandemic has peaked. After going to great heights in the bomb mirage, it is now beginning to come crashing down. The surge of the rift effect in the northern hemisphere, forced by the power of Britain, will now tilt towards Turkey before crossing into India and finally China.

There, the preparations for the eclipse shall begin with the neutralization of the coronavirus, acclimatising the energy from the Chinese experience to release energy for its journey into space.

The happening in the western hemisphere will be totally different. A folding from South America will engulf the north, with it then rolling across the Pacific Ocean to meet with outliers there and fusing as one for the journey.

Any outliers shall be collected for both camps on the collection pods heading for the outwards departure from Earth's atmosphere.

P.S., It is very important that people stay calm. This is an unprecedented spectacle, so it must not be read as a preference towards some foreign power.

VACCINE #1

In 1902, in Lexington, Alabama, in a biology laboratory, a specimen was created by Professor Graham Pullman. The good professor was a weird-looking man who did not seem to smile much.

I am with another group of specimens in a petri dish. On the opposite table, there is a row of different-sized specimens in petri dishes. One by one, we are fed to the other side until I am the only one left. I have reconciled myself to being next.

But the professor does not feed me to the others. He consoles my antigens with a form of matter which creates fusion. Then when done, he places me in a glass tube and corks it. He then picks up a vial containing nitro-glycerine and throws it hard at an adjacent wall. He runs out through the hole that it created. Upon turning around, he sees two security guards chasing him. He stumbles, then uncorks the tube, and throws me out. Then the two guards lead the professor away.

I suppose you want to know what my fusion read. It was in two parts per antigen.

'You must find the cure even if you must destroy the planet,' he said, so I did.

Over time, while fusing about and bouncing, I had many adventures like riding beetles, earwigs, ants, and dragonflies. In return, I helped move stuff and forage.

One time, I bounced onto a wire between two pylons, and a mirage of a site of the specimens I had seen in the petri dishes was coming towards me.

P.S., I am Cosmos. You are welcome.

ONE YEAR ON

It is now December 2020, one year after the coronavirus was detected on the planet. The numbers read 64,313,855 worldwide infected and 1,489,501 dead.

The five leading countries for infected and dead are as follows:

United States: 64,313,855 infected, 1,489,501 dead

Brazil: 6,388,526 infected 173,862 dead

India: 9,499,710 infected, 138,159 dead

Mexico: 1,122,362 infected, 106,765 dead

United Kingdom: 1643,086 infected, 59,051 dead

The planet's economies are in chaos. The stock markets that instantly crashed when the pandemic hit are increasingly trying to lie their way out by saying that the economies of countries are growing when nobody can afford to buy anything.

They are selling stocks at exorbitant values when they could not be worth half of said value. They make claims that stocks are good, and by week's end, they are useless.

Nations around the world are claiming greater than normal poverty numbers, and with the virus, they are ignoring the safety measures and opening their economies. Take America as an example, with the number of infected and dead way out of control.

Around the world, hospitals are inundated with very sick people and bed shortages, and the workers are overwhelmed and suffering from anxiety. There are claims of insufficient personal protection equipment (PPE) by frontline workers. Many people are unable to cope with the situation, which is causing depression, stress, and drug and alcohol abuse. Domestic abuse, crime, and suicide are also on the rise.

Area lockdowns are being implemented to try to slow the virus. But when the lockdown is lifted, the virus starts up at a rapid pace again.

The only good news is the said discovery of a vaccine. But when we will have access to said vaccine is anyone's guess! The end of the year has been mentioned, as has early next year (2021), the middle of next year, and late autumn of next year.

VACCINE #2

On 9 November 2020, a pharmaceutical company based in Germany, Pfizer, claimed to have discovered a vaccine for coronavirus with a 90 per cent success rate. The vaccine has to be stored at −80°C (−103°F) or its molecules lose their effectiveness. Two doses are required. Pfizer has started selling stocks on the stock exchange.

Moderna, a US biotech firm, says it has a vaccine that is 94% per cent accurate in curing COVID-19. The vaccine has to be stored at −20°C (−4°F). Of 15,000 given a placebo, 90 got sick from coronavirus. Of 15,000 given the drug, 5 got sick from coronavirus. Two doses are required. Moderna stocks rise on the stock exchanges.

Russia says its Gamaleya (Sputnik V) coronavirus vaccine is 92 per cent effective and can be stored at regular fridge temperature. Two doses are required. Stocks were floated on the stock market.

On 9 October 2020, a COVID-19 vaccine being made by AstraZeneca, in collaboration with Oxford University, was given first approval after part testing. On 23 October, AstraZeneca said the vaccine was up to 90 per cent effective. After questions about effectiveness, it was downgraded to 62–90 per cent effective. It needs regular fridge temperature for storage. Two doses are required.

On 1 December 2020, both Moderna and Pfizer apply for approval of their vaccine. Gamaleya has also applied for approval of worldwide distribution.

VACCINE #3

In December, the United Kingdom, Canada, the United States, Mexico, and Israel initiated a nationwide inoculation program using the Pfizer vaccine. The European Union began a rollout of the Pfizer vaccine.

China obtained a supply of the Pfizer vaccine. China's medical authorities agreed to allow a nationwide vaccination using the homemade vaccine by Sinopharm.

Malaysia bought doses of the Sinavac vaccine from China.

Argentina received consignment of Russia Gamaleya (Sputnik V) vaccine.

The US Federal Drug Administration (FDA) gave emergency authorisation for distribution of the Moderna vaccine.

Canada authorised use of the Moderna vaccine.

Data on the AstraZeneca and Oxford vaccine has been sent to the United Kingdom medical board for examination, seeking certification for use.

The UK Medicines and Health Regulatory Agency (MHRA) approved the Oxford and AstraZeneca vaccine.

Countries around the world were becoming concerned about a surge of the virus, which was being widely recognised as a third wave.

Countries in Europe were going into lockdown for December, including Italy, Germany, Holland, and the Czech Republic.

A new variant of the virus was discovered in the United Kingdom, which accelerated the virus's spread.

A second new variant was discovered that was said to have come from South Africa.

Countries around the world began to isolate the United Kingdom. The new variant of the virus began to show up around the world.

Track and trace was a hot topic with questions about why it was so effective in South Korea, China, Australia, and New Zealand yet was such a failure in the United States and the United Kingdom.

Children between the ages of eleven and fifteen were considered to be major carriers who were asymptomatic (no symptoms but could spread the virus).

BEGIN TO END

It is now January 2021, and the number of people on the planet who are infected is 100,331,754; the number of dead is 2,150,951.

The vaccination of the world has been activated, but it has been said that not until 2024 will the vaccine reach all corners of the planet.

On Monday, 4 January 2021, the first doses of the Oxford and AstraZeneca vaccine were given out in the United Kingdom.

India has approved two vaccinations, Bharat Biotech and AstraZeneca.

The European Medicines Agency agreed to use the Moderna vaccine.

There are three strains of the virus now on the planet: one that plugs the breathing, one that plugs and rips at the breathing, And one that plugs the breathing and closes down injured body parts where applicable. Each variant is more contagious than the previous. A new strain of the virus has been discovered in Brazil which is said to be similar to the UK and South American variants.

The infectious rate of the virus is spreading around the planet so quickly that scientists now say it is a race between the rate of spreading and the speed at which the vaccine can be distributed.

Every day, a record number of people are being infected. Hospitals around the world say that capacity is near the breaking point.

P.S., A good indicator that the vaccine is working will be when the number of infections starts to go down.

EFFECT #1

It is now July 2021, and the number of people infected is 186,491,983; the number who have died is 4,029,250.

There are different kinds of vacancies being used around the world. Pfizer and BioNtech in Germany. Moderna and Johnson & Johnson in America. AstraZeneca/Oxford in the United Kingdom. Gamaleya (Sputnik V) in Russia. Sinovac in China.

In April 2021, an organisation called COVAX was founded by the World Health Organization to help get vaccines to third world countries.

In March and April 2021 the pandemic started to again wreak havoc throughout Europe, India, and Brazil. the world is now looking to the vaccines to find a way out of this disastrous situation.

There is controversy between medical organisations. There is uncertainty about the Johnson and Oxford vaccines causing blood clots and about the Moderna are Pfizer vaccines causing heart inflammations.

Different variants of the virus are appearing all over the world. The South Africa variant is said to be able to break down the Pfizer vaccine. A Vietnam variant is a cross between the UK and India variants. The Brazil variant is causing horrific consequences in South America, killing more people in Brazil than are being born.

The India variant, also known as the Delta variant, is said to be very aggressive and spreading very quickly. At the moment, it is known as the dominant variant.

It is now more than six months into the year, and they have not stopped the spread of the virus. The good news is they have broken the link between infection and death; with each wave, far fewer are dying.

Indonesia, Russia, and the continent of Africa reported a surge in the virus caused by the Delta variant.

It has recently come to light that the more movement of people, the greater the spread of the contagion. The people getting infected are those who have not been vaccinated.

There has been talk in the United Kingdom about preparing a booster shot if needed. The Pfizer vaccine is said to be weakening months after injected, so the manufacturer is trying to develop a booster shot.

EFFECT #2

It is now January 2022. The number of people infected by the virus is 292,800,000, and the number who have died is 5,500,000. What has happened over the past twelve months? With the discovery of a vaccine, countries around the world have found the confidence to open up. After what many refer to as normality in the post-pandemic era, doctors have reported a lot of cases of what is known as long COVID, where people who have had the virus still feel the symptoms such as tiredness, difficulty breathing, and chest pains.

Countries are issuing vaccination certificates to those who have been fully vaccinated. Many countries will not accept foreigners unless they have been fully vaccinated. Workplaces are saying their employees must get vaccinated or lose their jobs. Only the vaccinated are allowed into places where there are large crowds such as nightclubs, festivals, theatres, and sporting events. Many demonstrations are occurring where people are claiming their civil rights are being violated. Different ways are being used to track the virus. COVID vaccination pop-up centres are being set up, as well as virus testing centres.

Lateral flow test kits for self-testing have been made available. An app for your phone has been set up to inform you if you come into contact with someone with the virus. Track and trace systems are being used to locate people who have been known to have been in contact with an infected person.

In May, children started receiving the COVID-19 vaccine. Children as young as five years old are being vaccinated. Also, children are recognised as major spreaders. The number of children getting infected from the virus is rising. The Delta variant has spread around the planet very rapidly, and vaccines seem to be holding in a way that many people are getting infected, but deaths are diminishing where countries have prioritized a vaccination program. However, other countries are still suffering.

In June, a new variant of the Delta variant, called Delta+, was discovered in Switzerland.

Because of the severity of the virus surge, many nations are enforcing safety protocols. Hospitals are reporting an increase of younger people being infected, as well as vaccinated people. Some nations are beginning to offer booster shots after the discovery that the efficacy of the vaccine begins to wane after a certain time. In July, Israel was the first nation to offer booster shots. In September, the United States became the first nation to start a mandate on vaccinations. In November, Novavax in the United States and Covaxin in India were given recognition as a vaccine against COVID- 19.

The first antiviral pill, made by Merck UK, called Molnupiravir, was given authorisation for use against the coronavirus. Russia has three single-shot vaccines: EpiVacCorona (December 2020), CoviVac (February 2021), and Sputnik Light (November 2021).

The virus surge is becoming very intense, so countries are panicking and offering booster shots of different makes to supplement their original shots, probably because it is the vaccine easiest to obtain. Countries are targeting those who do not want the vaccine by applying lockdowns or restricting what they can do. There are demonstrations and riots throughout Europe and the West Indies over COVID rules. Some countries enforce a full lockdown, and others used partial lockdowns, curfews, or safety protocols. The European Union gave a nine-month value on vaccination for travel. Some countries made vaccinations compulsory.

A new variant of the COVID-19 virus, given the name Omicron, has been found in Botswana, Africa. It is now December, and Omicron is the dominant variant of the coronavirus. The variant is so contagious that there are mass queues to get a booster shot, which is said to give the best protection against Omicron. Festivities for the holiday season are being heavily disrupted. Pfizer's antiviral pill, Paxlovid, which will help protect against the symptoms of COVID-19, is given recognition for use. Turkey has been given emergency recognition for their coronavirus vaccine Turkovac. There are nine countries at present that produce vaccines against the coronavirus.

EPILOGUE

What has been learnt over the years about the coronavirus?

- Defences against the virus.
    - Keep a distance from other people.
    - Ware a face mask.
    - Wash hands more often.
    - Stay at home.
    - Have windows open when possible.
    - Go out only to buy supplies.
    - Exercise only in a local area.
- Only key businesses are allowed to open (medical personnel, food and drink establishments).
- Essential maintenance workers include and fire and police personnel.
- During the height of the pandemic, all retail outlets, cinemas, sports centres, entertainment and festival places, and leisure and exercise centres closed. Holiday gatherings at home and abroad were banned.
- When a vaccine was discovered, lockdowns were eased, but then it was necessary to lockdown again when waves of the virus struck.
- The strain on the economy has been immense, with many places going bankrupt and closing down. When lockdown was eased, it was a gradual opening. First, only takeaway was allowed for pubs, cafés, and restaurants. Then there was opening of retailers with only so many people inside. Places that managed to stay open were having trouble with having to open and close again because of virus surges, as well as finding staff. Fully opening the economy did not begin until July 2021.

- Schools had been closed, and at the height of the pandemic, only home learning was allowed.
- Children of key workers were allowed in school throughout the pandemic.
- Office workers have been working from home. Only when lockdown has been stopped completely would they return to the offices.
- More people around the world are suffering from hunger. Prices for food and drink, petroleum, and housing have all risen.

BIOLOGICAL WARFARE

In December 2019, a biological warhead was exploded in China. Within four months, the whole planet was infected, and people were dying from the covis virus.

Since the initial attack, humanity has been hit continuously by different variants of the virus.

In 2021, different vaccines were discovered, and the fighting back had begun.

The explosion of the Delta biological warhead in India in June 2021 has had drastic consequences all over the world. It infects all before it—children, teenagers, young adults, and adults.

The fighting back has remained strong in countries where vaccination programs have been prioritized. Infections are very high in the unvaccinated, but deaths have gone down.

The virus war is very savage, with tens of thousands getting infected every day.

Both those vaccinated and those who are unvaccinated are falling victim to the virus, but with the discovery of a vaccine, those being hit mainly by the virus are those not vaccinated.

The future is uncertain, with the efficacy of the vaccine deteriorating after a period. It is possible that the virus could become immune to the vaccine. It's a dangerous world, and depending on a quick out is doubly dangerous.

P.S., What has been said may be fictional, but as the days have turned to years, they have seemed all too real.

TERRIFYING THOUGHTS

After reading my thesis, I have come to this conclusion. The newfound variant Lambda, found in Peru, is a sleeper and is the neuron frontline of the next big change in the coronavirus change.

I came to the conclusion that this effect would not happen for eight or nine years. I have not persuaded others of this process because if the variant does make such a massive change, then I think it will be a mass attack on different parts of the nervous system. If this happens, the effects of the known coronavirus will be different, with a clearer observance of the virus.

We must be careful in our preparation and not think that the drugs we use in the year 2021 will be all we need in the year 2030 to fight the virus.

P.S., A scientist with connections to Oxford/AstraZeneca and Portadown is saying the virus will then just go away. Does that mean the human race fades out? That the human race's way of thinking changes? What is recognised as the human race survives?

CORONAVIRUS

PERFECT STORM

Today's date is 24 September 2021.

On 20 August 2021, I was taken to the hospital and diagnosed with COVID-19. Back in approximately 2005, I was diagnosed with chronic obstructive pulmonary disease (COPD), which prevents oxygen from entering past the throat. So with the virus, I created the perfect storm.

Problem #1: I would not accept the oxygen. I kept saying not enough oxygen, no oxygen, and I couldn't breathe. So I had to go from the recovery unit to the intensive care unit (ICU), where I was given a full face mask. When I settled down, I was transferred to the lung recovery unit.

Problem #2: I got a sore throat and lost my voice. It felt like my throat was on fire. When I had my mask off, I was continuously coughing up phlegm. It was not until 20 September 2021 that I started to recover.

Problem #3: Once my stats for the virus were clear, I could hardly walk. Every effort was leaving me breathless. My energy levels were at ground zero, so the recovery was bit by bit.

The drugs they gave me were steroids, sleepers, a pill for my sore throat, antibiotics, nebulizers to further help with my breathing, paracetamol, and an injection every evening to stop blood clots.

On 24 September 2021, I was discharged from the hospital to recuperate at home.

P.S. Don't get the virus. Stay safe.

MATCH

Welcome, ladies and gentlemen, boys and girls, to Venom Stadium and the biggest match of the century. The two teams, Vaccine Injects and Virus Variants, are sure to give you the best excitement you can imagine.

The referees for this match are Mr Distance, Mr Mask, and Mr Window.

Here are the team players.

Team Vaccine: Pfizer, Germany

Jannsen, United States

Sputnik V, Russia

Sinovac, China

Sinopharm, China

AstraZeneca, United Kingdom

Moderna, America

Covaxin, India

Covishield, India

Zydus Cadila, India

Novavax, United States

Team Virus: Beta, South America

Gamma, Brazil

Lambda, Peru

Alpha, United Kingdom

Delta, India

Delta+, Switzerland

Coronavirus

COVID

Covis

Mutations

Symptoms

Well, that is the final whistle, and what a game it was. You could not get more excitement than that. At the moment, they are tallying up the score. The result will be made public as soon as it is known.

P.S., No substitutes were used in this match because the result is absolute.

REVIVAL

The date I was discharged from hospital was 24 September 2021. My energy levels were very low when I was released. When I got home, I could hardly walk. I was given pills for my throat and some sleeping pills.

One thing that bothered me while in hospital was that because I had such a sore throat, when my family phoned, I could not talk to them. Neither could I phone out.

The doctor warned me that getting my energy levels up to normal would be a long, slow process. I used all the pills for my throat, a month's supply, before my throat was better.

I was very lucky to have good neighbours because for the first few weeks, I did not have the strength to go to the shops and get supplies. I moved around my studio flat at a snail's pace.

Then when I felt better, I tried going to the shops, which turned out to be a big struggle. I had to stop three or four times to rest. When I got home, I was gasping for breath. After one month, I finally managed to walk down town and back without stopping to rest, but I still felt out of breath.

It is now 1 November 2021, and I feel I can get on my bike. Next month, I will go back in the gym. The symptoms I felt were my lungs not getting much oxygen, prick-like stings in my toes and sometimes on my back, and having to take deep breaths when I walked.

On 30 September 2021, I had to go to the post office. I tried to walk non-stop downtown but did not make it. I had to stop every so often.

I was exhausted all the way there and back. How strange is that after lazing about for nigh on a week?

On 6 October 2021, I managed to have a shower and do my laundry. I went to the bank and did a little shopping, but I still needed to rest three times. With a bit of luck, my lungs good, but I still need to catch my breath.

On 20 October 2021, I am still feeling breathless and groggy on my feet. I managed to walk to town and back without taking a rest.

P.S., It is now 17 November 2021, and my health status is very good. I do not think there is anything I cannot sort out with some exercise. Concerning the virus, I have been fortunate to not have had some kind of nasty aftereffect.

SUPER EXTINCTION

It is the year 2025, and the virus is stronger than it has ever been. I am not trying to place fault; the vaccines were no match for the intensity of the virus. The weather is terrible, with apocalyptic storms raging and snow falling in places which previously had tropical climates. Animals, birds, insects—are all suffering.

Word is getting around that we are about to suffer what is called an ice age.

If my intelligence is right, the poles are going to create what is called a neuron vortex, where an imaginary line connects between the two poles. It will then fluctuate until it has enough energy. Then after dispersing, they will divide and move at subsonic speed east and west around the planet, sucking up the virus to create their survival course. When the two entities meet again, they will disperse into minute particles. The energy dispersed into the survivors should leave them with the vaccine antibodies to show them how to survive a coronavirus onslaught.

P.S., I have never believed in weak vaccines. Vaccines are supposed to be the cure. Pumping false beliefs into your body will destroy you eventually.

FALLOUT

It is 2022, more than two years since the virus was located in Wuhan China. The health and economy of the world have major problems. The health services of countries around the world are being over stretched. Countries are saying they have inadequate skilled personnel or inadequate medical equipment.

Economies are struggling with the price of food going up, docks being blocked with ships unable to unload, a shortage of skilled truck drivers, and fuel, gas, and electricity prices going up. Workers are demanding higher wages. One of the problems about getting the vaccine is people being sceptical and believing misinformation. Many people believe when you get the virus, you produce antibodies, which are physically produced and so give real protection. That is true, but what about variants? The problem with creating vaccines so quickly is that problems are being found after they have been given the go-ahead to be unleashed on the public. The AstraZeneca vaccine is being accused of causing blood clots. The Pfizer and Moderna vaccines are accused of causing heart issues.

Many people who have been (double) vaccinated are being admitted to hospital with the virus. The vaccine and immune system have weakened! When you are given a booster shot because your immune system has weakened, does that mean you are creating a dangerous situation in the immune system that could cause the creation of a new coronavirus strain? Vaccine boosters are being given, so after receiving a booster shot, you shall need added booster shots down the line! When you inject too much of something, you need more for the same effect, so will that situation occur? That is why vaccines go through a severe testing program of seven to ten years to ensure there are no side effects.

Problems occur when you are not taking into consideration that diseases attack the immune system and try to nullify its properties. With this new variant called Omicron and its ability to spread, are we signalling an atmospheric covis change in which the antigens devise a strategy and multiply?

On a more pleasant note, with the creation of an antiviral drug, it has become easier to fight the virus. On a sour note, the problem with the pill is there is a short window (three to five days) in which the drug can be given for effectiveness before the virus takes hold.

P.S., Until there is a vaccine that can give us antibodies and absolutely eradicate COVID-19 from our bodies, humanity will have to continue to persist as best it can and face the heartache of continued high numbers of infections and deaths.

IS OR IS NOT

Warning

Do not get hit on the head by falling acorns this autumn, or you could catch the coronavirus. (It had to be said.)

COVID Advice

Survivor: I've been turned upside down, inside out, and stretched this way and that. What do I do now?

Human: You emancipate all your holdings and give them to me!

Cabinet of Treasure

As the New Wave junkies look at all the different vaccines and pills (over a dozen) used in the fight against coronavirus, they think, *Have I got enough?*

Legend of the Covis Pirate

Dig me artie the treasure be here.

Cap'n, I found sumit. It be a phone with that message fingy.

Shiver me timbers, waud it says?

It says, 'You have been tested positive, so must isolate.'

OMO

No to Corona

(Cool billboard or what)

Blooming

The Cure for Coronavirus

Drink one full glass of Corona soft drink every day until bottle is empty. (There is no virus in Corona, so it will go away.)

Resume

Name:	Corni Cropper
Address:	Coffee Falls
	Virus Square
	Planet Conquered
Occupation:	Survivor
Hobbies:	Truth and Consequences
Credentials:	Past Life

Message to the World
You have covis, so live with it,
Because it will not live with you.

COVID-19 FORUM

One of the things noticed about the new wave junkies is that they have moved from injecting to pill popping.

Covis Symptoms
Interviewer: 'Hello, folks. Welcome to downtown Galactica, outside the Metropolis vault. We are here to get the lowdown at one of the biggest heists ever, over 750,000,000 egots. Our eyewitness is a Miss Daisy May. Miss May, can I call you Daisy?'

Interviewee: 'Yes, certainly.'

Interviewer: 'Daisy, in your own words, what did you see?'

Interviewee: 'It was awful. This armed robber walked in with what looked like different size needles. I could only see him from a distance, you understand. Its face looked like a ghost, and it said, 'What do we have here?' Then everybody looked at him as if going weak, and their faces looked like ice. Some started to choke and cough, trying to catch their breath. Then, looking like nothing, the robber spoke to the tellers one by one. They struggled to understand its words. It then blew the safe, with bloody repercussions that showed the inside. When finished, the robber then fired the needles—I mean guns, hitting almost everyone. While leaving, it covered its tracks by releasing a toxic canister. It was terrible, like everyone's worst nightmare.'

Interviewer: 'Yes, thank you. So, guys, what next?'

PRECAUTIONS

Here is a list of precautions used to stop the COVID-19 virus from spreading.

- Wear a mask to prevent breathing in the virus.
- Keep space between others.
- Wash your hands with soap more often.
- Put your hand over your mouth when coughing.
- Put your hand over your nose and mouth when sneezing.
- Open a window to disperse virus particles.
- Clean surfaces with disinfectant.
- Use aerosols.
- When a person dies, burn the body.
- Avoid large crowds.
- Get vaccinated against the virus.
- Use antiviral pill protection against the virus.
- Isolate when in contact with infected.
- Isolate if infected.
- Take an official test for the virus.
- Try home testing kits.
- Wear gloves when lifting in unfamiliar areas.
- Follow a total lockdown except for key workers.
- Follow a partial lockdown of infected areas.
- Close the national borders.
- Administer curfews.
- Disallow international travel.
- No hugging.
- No kissing.

- Ban festivities.
- Allow only certain numbers into activities.
- Require vaccine passports for entry to places.
- Deny unvaccinated entry to places.
- Wear a mask when boarding public transport.
- Show a vaccine passport when boarding public transport.
- Show a vaccine passport when boarding an airplane.
- Work from home.
- Quarantine nations of concern.
- Make any or all of the above mandatory.

WAR WORLD

As the boy lies under the bed sheets with only a torch for light, he reads his comic book. A biological bomb has been dropped on Germany, and Europe is under heavy attack, with devastating consequences.

The government of Merck has quickly sent out its forces of Molnupiravir capsules. But the vaccine command centre is getting hit with such force that it has had to bring up reinforcements. So into the fray is sent a mixture of commando vaccines, Pfizer, Moderna, and Johnson, which are ordered to shoot anyone and everyone in sight of their syringes.

But still the virus attacking force devastates humanity's front line, with such savagery spilling into neighbouring nations.

The vaccine command tries a new tactic in a desperate effort to stem the influx of the virus force. People who have not been vaccinated are ordered to stay at home under lockdown except for work, exercise, and sustenance.

One paramedic says to the other, 'I can see the papers tomorrow. Now we must fight or die until we get through this.'

As the infected are rushed to hospital, the body count rises.

Approximately two weeks later, the United States reports that a biological bomb has been unleashed on the state of Oklahoma, and quickly the virus spreads. But this time the United States initiates some kind of defence: masks, distance, and curfews. The vaccine guards are quickly sent out, shooting all and urging civilians to get shot. But reports at vaccine command say the virus enemy is breaking out, spreading forth, and blasting outlying states.

The Moderna vaccine army is on high alert.

The Pfizer marines are preparing to launch a planned attack with their Paxlovid capsules. Outlying entrenched vaccine forces in Asia have reported being under sustained attacks.

The virus command has sent out a warning over the airwaves, telling the different vaccines not to do anything stupid.

P.S., The infection battle seems to be going on forever. Suddenly the vaccine's front line is attacked by a variant hoard, creating agony beyond compare as if ripping it apart and putting it together again (antibodies energy).

The vaccine shouts, 'Lucky I am full of it.' Then the virus looks and attacks again but, having no variation on the attack, fades away.

I know I should act like a hero for drawing it in, away from the others, but all I feel is drained and shell-shocked. The truth is I feel like the luckiest capsule alive. That was some space bomb.

OPERATION

'Well, Doctor, the X-ray shows we shall definitely have to operate.'

'Yes, Doctor, I absolutely agree. Nurse, please prepare the patient for surgery and inform the team.'

'Hello, sir. We expect the surgery to proceed without complications. You will be good as new when you awake.'

'Anaesthetist, please, so we can proceed?'

'First, ladies and gentlemen, I shall cut him open. I shall now align the plasma can, ventricle, and neonolical in that order. There, that is successfully done. Nurse, would you wipe my forehead, please?'

'I am now going to connect the nerve line to the neurone system. What the …? Doctor, do not touch it anymore. I suggest we clear the area. The surgery is a mess, and we all have to change—it has got all over you. Agreed? Leave the patient; he is gone for sure. I have to speak to the director.'

'Sir, we have a problem. An operation has just gone awry.'

'Oh, dear. I am the director of this hospital, so it must not be that big. What is this problem?'

'Well, I tried to make a connection, and it exploded. Now every time I touch, it expands, and it might be contagious.'

'My God. Doctor, what do you suggest we do?'

'It's spreading so fast, it must be on the outskirts of town by now.'

'It's what? Go make your report, and don't forget to pronounce the patient dead. I have to report to the United Nations and try to explain that the end of the world is not a bad thing.'

'Doctor, before you go, is there any money in it?'

'UN, is that all you have to say?'

'Well, sir, I guess that does prove how big the neurone system is.'

P.S., The hospital was an eerie place made of big, solid brick with archaic-looking surgery instruments inside. It stood on its own in a wasteland and looked so cool when shown getting demolished in the newspaper.

My name is Keith Radmall.

I was born in September in the city of
Coventry, in the Midlands of Britain.

I left school when I was fourteen years old and then had no
form of education until 2013, where I used various educational
institutions to get four GCSEs (IT, science, maths, English).

I have never married and have no children.

I have had various jobs: kitchen porter, club centre
cleaner, exhibition centre, and more.

I have travelled extensively around Europe and America.

I am a bit of a collectorholic and have various collections.

Stonehenge:

I look at the crowd with no sight on me.
I walk towards, into, and through the stone.
My thought is, I care not; I shall not return.

Vision.

COVID-19

OMICRON

The Omicron variant of the coronavirus was discovered in Botswana, Africa, in November 2021. The variant is considered to be a very fast spreader. Countries are tightening their borders and bringing in restrictions. Scientists around the world are getting nervous about the new variant. It seems the variant doubles its number of infections every two to three days. Omicron is said to resist vaccines, is highly evasive, and is causing infections at an alarming rate. Vaccine laboratories say they will be able to tweak their vaccines to combat the Omicron variant. Symptoms of the variant so far have been mild: dry cough, scratchy throat, muscle aches, colds, and fatigue.

Korea claims it has found a stealth variant of the Omicron strain, meaning it is difficult to trace. Scientists say they have found a stealth variant of Omicron that is undetectable by regular (PCR) testing. The variant is very virile, meaning it quickly saturates the oxygen in the body and makes you feel very weak. The problem with this is the body goes into a flatline scenario. Then the variant has a line to the brain, and thus manipulation takes place. Where the mind is very complicated, the variant turns the pulse over; that is, the mind thinks sad, but the variant senses happy and sends a pulse of happy. The variant will continue to do this until the victim dies, is rendered COVID free, or virus antigens are fused. Upon sensing a connection break, it will explode. This occurrence will create a foreboding of terror: your mind explodes, taking you as body particles. All the time leading up to the blast, it was like a foreboding of something to happen.

I recognised it as nothing because its final outcome showed an aura of consequences. Then it was a sense of what will be shall be.

Beware the Omicron. It is not weak—it is a ticking bomb. Because it has a base particle of fatigue, it will collect particle compounds of other variants. When agitated, it will explode. The victims of circumstances must remain in stealth. This is your time bomb.

Science fiction or not?

P.S., This is a discovery that the variants of COVID-19 are interconnected. organisation.

TOXIC

As I walk towards the wagon train, I drop to the ground. This is the end for me, I think.

Then I hear, Get me some water—it looks almost dead. You must listen; it is coming. My name is Omiton. Good, it's choking. Here, have a shot of this.

The wave, the surge, you must be aware it is coming.

Steady. You've got a fever and look to be in pain.

From beyond, do not sleep. The nightmare is real; it eats you alive again and again. When you awaken, you will feel like another part of you is missing. Forgive me. Drink yourself silly. Keep your mind clear. It's coming, the surge. It wants so much until you have nothing else to give. Then you die for not being kind and giving.

You must stay alive, survive, or there is nothing to live for, and it will see and give you more.

The agony, the nightmare, it is coming from more, for more. Live, or you shall die. Don't let it find you. You must burn my body, release my spirit.

You must promise me: make it, be of yourself. Sigh …

It's gone—delusions of grandeur, dribblings of a madman.

I wonder what is out there. What do you think? I don't know nuts!

There is something that he said. Nah, the heat got it; just delusional. Anyway, we must hurry if we are going to reach the next town before sundown to have a jar. Don't you mean play some poker?

Too true, yae neddy.

Farther along the journey: What is that bright light? I have no idea. Unhitch your horse, and let's look. Wow, look at the headdress. What is the writing? Go fetch the scout; I'll wait here. Johnny, what's it say?

In Cheyenne it says, 'Here lies unworldly treasures.' Let's look in the cave!

Wow, what an eerie place. Casket barrels in the wall, and an Indian skeleton with a weapon with each. Scout, how long before we reach the coast?

I'd say a year, eleven months at a push.

Good enough. We'll take the barrels and get the herbalist to conjure up some brew.

In the mountains, before the last leg of the journey, Jimmie opens the liquor. A strange silence overcomes them. Then the trail boss sees Rich stand up. Then with a look of the devil in his eyes, he pulls his gun. Boss shouts out, 'Stop!' Rich fires three shots before Boss pulls his gun and shoots the gunner dead. Three people lie dead, and the survivors shake their heads.

At the meeting the next day, the boss says, 'My sympathy to you folks who lost loved ones. If it is any consolation, there will be no more Indian liquor on this trail.'

P.S., Mind of the trail scout: There is no war paint. What are they, Iroquois (peace), Apache (warrior), or whatever?

Mind of the trail boss: I'm so sorry, Mrs Green, but I had to put him down or he would have killed us all.

LOOMING CHAOS

- Hospitals overwhelmed with patients suffering from the virus. Inadequate supplies to work sufficiently and safely. Lack of oxygen containers.
- Industry and hospitality having to go into lockdown because of virus surge.
- The strain on the banks to cover the cost of the pandemic.
- Schools having to close because of the virus spreading in pupils and teachers.
- Price hikes causing people to struggle paying for necessities.
- Governments taking people's rights away and using the virus as the excuse.
- Only so many clients allowed into establishments.
- Difficulty in finding employees who want to work in a pandemic atmosphere.
- Many small businesses having to close down because of lockdowns and the virus.
- Sports programs being postponed or having to take place behind closed doors; spectators must have a COVID passport.
- People paying for functions and then having to cancel or limit the number of guests because of lockdown and security instructions.
- Businesses having to police their facilities or face a fine, which increases overhead costs.
- Companies forcing employees to get vaccinated against the virus or face getting fired.
- People wanting to go on holiday, but different countries require different vaccine certification or requirements, which can cost a lot of money on top of holiday costs.

- Limit on how many people can visit old people in care homes.
- Advised-against party celebrations.
- Festive activities interrupted.
- The longer the pandemic goes on, the more the financial burden there is on establishments.
- Companies are on lockdown or choose to work from home, affecting surrounding workplaces that depend on their customers and staff.
- Many more people preferring to shop online than at the stores.
- People getting vaccinated and then being told that after a few months, they need a booster because the antibodies have waned.
- People not being able to live comfortably in a pandemic world because of the strain and costs.
- Greedy companies and people pricing products out of reach of common people.
- People do not know how long the virus will last. If people get the virus, will they be able to survive during and after?
- Queues to get booster shots because of waning vaccine or new variants of virus.
- People cancelling appointments and bookings because of virus severity.
- Insecurity for companies and people to pay their debts to carry on.
- How do you protect those who have no immune response to the vaccines?
- Being insecure because of difficulty understanding the rules and regulations.
- Non-observance of COVID regulations cause a fine to be implemented.

ABSORBING

As my journey around the universe comes to an end, I am plummeted with potonic incarnate.

A feeling of endless shots of corni hit me. My only sense is that I am done with it all.

Suddenly it stops, and I drift and come into a nucleus of variables. Then I am waiting to go explode and unleash a thankful end to someplace not wanted.

In the future, I look deep into my mind and see the travesty in the future that the coronavirus has caused. I then pick something up from amongst the chaos. It is not quite clear what it is, and it shall not be known until it fades.

In the motion, as the virus moves, the victim complains. The vision of world's end and the humans saying so gradually cause terrifying consequences.

For some reason, scientists and people are saying so without facts, causing heartache and worry to many, which is a clear sign of forcing the issue.

P.S., I have a plastered view of you. Please do not associate me with the human race.

FUTURE END

The vision before the end is coming towards me but is taking forever to arrive.

Then I see it. As it passes by, different particle compound upon it, and I realise the numerical value of the count was the same as the count of variants.

The sense of a gathering for the final outcome.

Understanding now, but will they understand in the far future?

The end of a nightmare, thank goodness for that.

I am asleep. I keep trying to force myself to awaken.

Finally I wake up, and I feel terrible, as if I have died.

I look up, see the white light, and know instantly it is a coronavirus endgame.

Reacting instinctively, I zap every star in range with, 'If we fall, we fall together.'

As the implosion occurs, I watch as the twinkles go out and we all fall.

I awaken from the faint, feeling as if I am in a sea of sweat and as if my heart has outlasted the rest of me. Then I very slowly stand up.

My thought here is, 'Get me some of that.'

Then I go have some breakfast. When walking outside, I can still feel the ferocity of the implosion. Alas, I may not be a giant, but I feel like one. Then I have sense to forget.

P.S., Thank you for seeing me to the finish of the forbidden end.

REPORTED VIEW

Politicians: Politics is very intricate, but when it comes to saving lives in an emergency situation, they are very unforgiving. They talk out of the top of their heads, saying we must do this and do that, but they forget it is an emergency, so they make things worse. They give hard-worked-for taxes away so people won't work, and then they wonder why all over the country, places close down and claim bankruptcy. They talk gibberish about things that don't exist anymore. If they do not exist, then they cannot have, so move on.

Vaccine Etiquette: Governments have pushed for people to get vaccinated against COVID-19. They have thrown efficacy out the window and then wonder why the vaccine tolerance is waning. Already it is from six months to ten weeks. Scientists are saying the vaccine will protect against the virus. That is because of their panicking and not giving science the chance to evolve. Employers are firing workers if they do not get vaccinated. Those who do not want the vaccine are being denied their freedom and liberty. For foreign travel, vaccine passports are becoming a part of the procedure.

Household: Families are suffering intolerable hardships, such as how many can get together and when they are allowed to work. Children are being affected by school closures and are trying to learn from home. Families then have to pay for babysitters because of work. Also, there is stress when family members have to work from home. Families are being forced to stay apart. Prices for food and drink are forcing families to struggle, causing them to make choices and go without when before, they could afford it. The price of fuel has skyrocketed, putting the lives of the elderly and vulnerable in danger. It is not possible for wages to keep up with such a high cost of living. Holidays are ruined because of airlines cancelling flights or costing thousands more because of virus and vaccine stipulations.

Entertainment and Hospitality: When people are asked to work from home, it affects the businesses that depend on them. Places are forced to open and close on government say-so. People are being refused entrance if they do not have a vaccination passport. Establishments have to pay for this security. Only so many people are being allowed into some establishments, which is causing financial difficulties. Places that are managing to stay open are barely able to break even. Many have a time limit on such costs or a procuring department, which has a lot to do with paying the wages of their employees.

Emergency Services: Hospitals, paramedics, doctors, and nurses are being put under immense pressure by the virus. Hospitals are becoming overcrowded with patients who have contracted the disease. Paramedics are collecting patients who then have to wait at hospitals because there are no vacant beds. Doctors are in constant danger from the deadly outcome of the virus after having to examine infected patients. Nurses are continuously having to monitor infected patients and rush to stressed patients. They are all having to work long shifts, sometimes more than twelve hours.

P.S., Key workers are always in danger of catching COVID-19. They never know when they shall meet a surge or cluster of the contagion. They work in food and drink, sewerage, security, roadwork, and more.

QUESTIONS AND ANSWERS

- What are the various symptoms of COVID-19?
  High temperature, continuous cough, loss of sense of smell and taste.

- Do different variants have different symptoms?
  Yes. For example, Omicron adds loss of appetite and vomiting.

- What are the variants' differences?
  Severity of variant, ability to spread.

- What variants are the strongest?
  Delta and Alpha are known to cause death.

- Dose tolerance control the severity of the disease?
  The immune system protects against the disease.

- Which variant has the longest hospitalization period when infected?
  Results vary.

- Which variant has killed the most people?
  Delta variant.

- Which variant spreads the quickest?
  Omicron variant.

- Can different variants infect a person at the same time?
  Yes.

- What is the best breeding ground for the virus?
  Room temperature and humidity of less than 50 per cent.

- Can you order the variants from weakest to strongest?
  Omicron, Lambda, Beta, Gamma, Alpha, Delta, Delta+.

- Is the virus transmitted by body contact, by air, or both?
  Through air particles into the mouth, nose, or eyes. Rarely from surfaces.

- Which season of the year is the virus most contagious?
  Winter.

- Can the virus live outside the body? If so for how long?
  It dies very quick under UV light: two hours to nine days depending on the surface.

- How long will the pandemic exist?
  Until it loses out to the immune system.

- Will the virus be with us forever?
  It is a known contagion. What will they want to know?

P.S., Omicron and influenza are both virus pandemics. The symptoms of both are very similar. Protection from both is wearing a face mask, but both are different pathogens, so they look different.

OBSERVATIONS

There are now three facts scientists are noticing about the coronavirus.

1. The surge is being spearheaded by the Delta and Omicron variants.
2. Hospitalizations with the virus are rising.
3. The Omicron variant infection rate is skyrocketing.

A good thing is the Omicron variant transmits only mild symptoms. Though infection rates are very high, death rates are decreasing.

Work capability of many companies is being affected with illness, and people have to isolate.

Schools are still being interrupted through staff and pupil sickness.

Matches of various sports are being cancelled because of infections to team members.

Airports are in chaos, with cancelations and staff shortages blamed on the virus. The advice is against taking a sea cruise because ships have to quarantine during outbreaks.

In South Africa, where the Omicron variant was discovered in November, they are now claiming the virus surge has peaked in their country.

A new disease called Flurona, which is a combination of coronavirus and influenza. has been detected in Israel.

A new COVID variant called IHU, with forty-six mutations, has been found in France. If it is not of concern, then what is?

A new COVID variant called Deltacron has been discovered in Cyprus. It is a combination of the Delta and Omicron variants. Some scientists say it is caused by cross-contamination.

Scientific data say it will not be possible to vaccinate people around the world every four to six months.

The pressure on hospitals keeps increasing, with staff absentees and lack of space for patients. Staff in Australia were asked to work even though they were infected. Hospitals are finding it more difficult to perform their duties, with non-emergency procedures having to be postponed. Military personnel are being used for medical support.

Reinfections with the coronavirus are becoming more common. Is that because of a waning immune system, or is virus able to avoid vaccine protection?

The Omicron variant is a vibrating neurocoele, which makes it seem like a weak covis contagion. That means it vibrates each antigen until it spikes. When it has fulfilled its quest and all antigens are equal, it will implode, thus spreading its damaging particles around the airwaves with devastating consequences.

P.S., My thought is, 'I am prepared.' I sleep in the light of knowledge, and when I awake, I walk maybe nine feet as I am drowned in a flood of the great pandemic.

I am standing and looking forward, after passing through a sea of grief and sorrow. The one speck of joy is I did survive.

VARIANTS AND VACCINES

Variants

Beta variant (B.1.351), discovered in South Africa, May 2020.

Alpha variant (B.1.1.7), discovered in United Kingdom, September 2020.

Delta variant (B.1.617.2), discovered in India, October 2020.

Lambda variant (C.37), discovered in Peru, South America, December 2020.

Mu variant (B.1.621), discovered in Columbia, South America, January 2021.

Gamma variant (P.1), discovered in Brazil, South America, January 2021.

Theta variant (P.3), discovered in the Philippines, February 2021.

Delta+ variant (AY.4.2.), discovered in Switzerland, June 2021.

IHU variant (B.1.640.2), discovered in France, November 2021.

Omicron variant (B.1.1.529), discovered in Botswana, Africa, November 2021.

Omicron subvariant (BA.2), discovered in South Africa, November 2021.

P.S., Since the beginning of the coronavirus pandemic, there have been different variants of the virus, each with varying ferocity of infection.

Vaccines

AstraZeneca vaccine, United Kingdom
Research name AZD 1222, registered November 2020
Vaccine type: non-replicating viral vector

Moderna vaccine, America
Research name mRNA 1273, registered December 2020
Vaccine type: RNA

Pfizer vaccine, Germany
Research name, BNT 162b2, registered December 2020
Vaccine type: RNA

Johnson & Johnson, Janssen vaccine, United States
Research name JNJ-78436735, registered December 2020
Vaccine type: non-replicating viral vector

Gamalya, Sputnik V, Russia
Research name DB15848, registered August 2020
Vaccine type: andenovirus viral vector

Gamalya, Sputnik light vaccine, Russia
Research name, registered May 2021
Vaccine type: viral vector

Health institute, Turkovac vaccine, Turkey
Research name NCT04942405, registered December 2021
Vaccine type: inactivated

Covaxin vaccine, India
Research name BBV152, registered November 2021
Vaccine type: inactivated

Sinopharm vaccine, China
Research name 2503126-65-4, registered May 2021
Vaccine type: inactivated

Sinovac aka CoronaVac, China
Research name DB15806, registered June 2021
Vaccine type: inactivated

Novavax, Nuvaxovid vaccine, America
Research name NVX-CoV2373, registered January 2022
Vaccine type: protein subunit vaccine

Zydus Cadila, India
Research name ZyCoV-D, registered January 2022
Vaccine type: nasal DNA plasmid base

Antiviral Pills

Pfizer, Germany
Research name Paxlovid, registered November 2021

Merck, United Kingdom
Research name Molnupiravir, registered December 2021

Virus Spray

Glenmark, India
Research name Nitro Oxide Nasal Spray (NONS), registered February
2022
Brand name FabiSpray

P.S., With the introduction of vaccines and antiviral pills to stop the pandemic, there have been various problems such as bad aftereffects, efficacy waning, and inability to contain various strains of the virus.

DEMISE

As COVID-19 keeps infecting people around the world, so far the world has been lucky, with hundreds of millions infected and the dead in only single-digit millions.

There is now a big worry on the front line with people getting vaccinated and getting a booster shot. A report has come in that says any more booster shots will not give much protection against the virus. There is talk that a silver bullet will be needed, but others say that is not going to be possible.

With the Omicron variant being the dominant variant and being the weakest, any new variant will be very bad.

There is also a bigger problem, with some countries on borderline war footing. the rich are getting richer and the poor are getting poorer, with skyrocketing prices and the virus being rampant around the world. All that is needed is for someone to step out of line, and the world will create a world-ending situation.

The world is getting scared of its own shadow, and it is getting hard to see how much more people can take.

In January 2022, a new subvariant, called the stealth variant of the Omicron, was discovered in the United Kingdom. It has been called the stealth variant because it takes a while to trace. It is now spreading across the planet. It has a faster growth rate than the original Omicron variant.

Countries around the world are starting to lift the restrictions used to try and stop the virus. It has been said that Omicron spreads so quickly, no safety measures can stop it. Truckers in Canada have started a movement against mandatory vaccinations when crossing borders, blocking roads in major cities and bridge crossings. These demonstrations have spread to other countries, including France and New Zealand.

It is now February. Even with lockdowns and precautions being reversed around the world, many countries are reporting spikes in infections and deaths. There are reports that the death rate is plateauing. With no detection of new variants, the world is able to gain some reprise and assess the damage. It is not looking good!

A new thought process of learning to live with the virus is being processed. If we do that, with the virus wanting to kill humanity, then who becomes the object of experimentation?

Israel, one of the most vaccinated countries in the world, has reported a surge in the number of people dying daily from the virus.

Glenmark Pharmaceuticals (India) introduced a nasal spray in the fight against the virus, a nitric oxide nasal spray (NONS) with the brand name FabiSpray.

P.S., Subvariants are cataclysmic multiples of different antigens from different COVID viruses which all have their own objective when making a viral contact surge.

PREDICTION

This report was written in January 2022 to mitigate a future instinct.

In July 2022, a new variant of the coronavirus was discovered. This variant is said to be very dangerous and is made up of various antigens of other variants. It is efficient in quickly infecting and can avoid the immune system by varying its antigen protocol when confronted, thus infecting at will.

In December, a cluster of variants was discovered that seemed to work together, procuring various attack sequences and making them hard to stop and destroy.

In June 2023, another new variant was found which has caused horror and terror at its capabilities. It is said that when it attacks, it annihilates the surrounding structure, thus creating a quick killing scenario.

A problem with vaccines is surfacing: if a vaccine is created, would it not be reversed by the effect of the coronavirus variant attack or cause a closing down of the immune system? With this discovery, a way of tainting the blood is being considered. I have called this the stretch effect, lasting for about three years.

P.S., The teenager says, 'I don't believe you. You're full of it.' Later: 'Look what is happening. Everyone is getting sick and dying. You have to stop it.' When this horrific occurrence happens and all feels lost, there must be a finding that can stop the virus and is easy to understand, meaning there is not much more damage COVID-19 can do.

SPLITTING THE ATOM

After receiving the information that an emergency message has arrived, I climb into my capsule. The message reads, 'Death is coming.' I switch off the sigmonitor and go outside. I then throw my mind. I am now in a scientist's laboratory, and he is looking at a chip on a microscope. As he looks, he is disturbed that the elements within are seething with change, not floating. After getting the chip from under the microscope, he places it in a lead holder and then leaves the room. In seventeen minutes, he returns carrying a cylinder labelled helium, which he then pours into a tank. After picking up the chip with some tweezers, he carefully places it in the tank of helium. Then he looks at the clock on the back wall and times how long it takes to dissolve. Three hours forty-two minutes later, he is satisfied and puts a sticker on the lid reading, 'Dispose Of.'

Suddenly, two men carrying handguns burst in through the back door and demand to know where the crystalline is. The professor says, 'You're too late. I have destroyed it.' Then he turns to run for the front door. One of the gangsters shoots him in the back, and they ransack the place, taking any papers they can find. When satisfied there is nothing else, they disappear the way they came.

I then float out of the front door and down a corridor until I find an exit outside. It is dark and quiet, so the scientist must have been working in secret.

I walk to the capsule and climb in. After checking the data, I set the controls for empty space. Once there, I align the capsule to spaceship mode.

As the Omicron variant encrusts the atmosphere of the planet, deep within its structure, the ultravariants make preparations to manipulate their antigens to ignite explosions of unknown magnitude and unleash another devastation on humanity. I am sitting in the spaceship and thinking, *This is it.* I put on my helmet, clip on to the ship, and raise the canopy. After moving towards the rogue satellite, I grasp an antenna and manoeuvre into position to open the bubble.

I look inside, see what I am after, and reach my hand towards it. I feel I am stretching myself limb from limb, but I grasp the chip and steadily remove it.

I put it into the electroze canister and ensure I close it firmly and double latch it. Then I place it in my space belt, close the bubble, and return to my spaceship.

Inside the ship, I make myself comfortable. Then I removed the canister from my belt, look at it for a moment, insert the code (4321), and disintegrate the chip within.

I set the controls for Earth and the pandemic battle on the planet.

P.S., I know I cannot stop the destiny of the planet. But I can stop COVID-19 from manipulating the future.

ENDORSEMENT

It is now February 2022. With the diminishing effect of the Omicron variant and no new variants developing, many countries have started a policy of 'living with coronavirus'. Reports from around the world have indicated a diminishing rate of infection and deaths. Security measures at the borders, such as a necessary negative test before entry or boarding of an airplane, are being relaxed so people can travel. Some countries are allowing you to enter without being fully vaccinated. Protection measures against the virus, such as wearing of a mask and distancing, have been lifted within many countries.

Large events such as concerts and sporting events no longer require proof of vaccination or that you have had the virus. Establishments no longer have to limit the number of persons allowed to enter. It is no longer necessary for people to take a self-test or to self-isolate if they come into contact with a person who tests positive.

Some countries have taken these measures because their economies cannot stand the pressure.

Strange observations of COVID include what doctors call long COVID, which is where a patient has recovered from the virus but has long-lasting ailments. When a patient has had a vaccine and is protected against the virus, then the vaccine wanes, and they catch the disease. The scientific finding is that you can have more than one form of the virus infecting you at the same time. An example is Deltacron, a cross between the Delta and Omicron variants.

This paragraph is a slow creating hypothesis, like déjà vu. Beware— the Omicron stealth variant and the Deltacron variant are hybrids. They have taken the energy format of Omicron. Like a bullet, it enters the human anatomy and then explodes, creating damaging contaminants within through replication and interference with damaged cells. They then eat their way through the host and acclimatise as if not ever being there. They are ready to materialise and succeed again in their next victim. A dangerous format provocation is the development of a concentrated, systematic attack when the hybrid format is saturated.

P.S., The WHO and many governments have advised people to proceed with caution.

CLANDESTINE

When a variant increases in number, sometimes it changes its active appearance, and this is what causes a new variant to materialise.

The Omicron B.2 variant, aka Omicron stealth variant, was found originally in South Africa and has proven to be highly evasive against vaccines. It is considered to spread the virus quicker than the original version. It is harder to detect and is more evasive against antibodies if you have had the virus previously. It has more variations than the original and is more distinct. Scientists say it should be labelled a variant of concern and be given its own Greek letter of the alphabet.

Scientists have come out saying that it is of vital importance that a super-long-lasting vaccine is discovered.

COVAX, created by the WHO and supported by UNICEF, is supplying vaccines to third world countries. It is also supporting poor countries to make their own vaccines against COVID-19.

With all the fever of COVID-19, scientists and the media have been acknowledging that the various virus variants have been trying to dominate each other. I would agree to disagree. I think the virus is a neuronic collective, and the different variants operate as a network so they can survive in the ever-changing atmosphere.

In March 2022, China, a country that has had zero tolerance against COVID-19, reported its highest daily infection rate, with Hong Kong being the most infected region. China is struggling to control an outbreak of the Omicron stealth and Deltacron variants!

With the waning of vaccines, the number of hospitalizations is increasing. The number of infections is also beginning to rise.

The WHO have come out with a statement that the Deltacron is recognised as a COVID variant and is beginning to spread. It has the ferocity of Delta and the spread effectiveness of Omicron, so it could become a variant of concern!

A report has been submitted that there could in fact be over eighteen million deaths from the coronavirus.

On 24 March 2022, the United States became the first country to register over one million deaths from COVID-19.

Some countries are starting to offer a fourth booster shot, such as Israel and England.

P.S., It is very worrying that you must get a booster shot after a certain time, given the thought that the immune system will get so weak, it transforms to the other side when being affected by different variants. Collective bargaining with such a force is no bargain.

DISASTROUS

The coronavirus began in Wuhan, China, in December 2019. It is now March 2022, and as the world takes a breath, like folding space, the virus epicentre is again in China, in the province of Hong Kong.

Days later, Korea and countries in Europe (Germany, Italy) report virus surges.

This time, the virus is proceeding at a far greater speed. Humanity braces for another worldwide attack of COVID-19. Once more into the breach.

Tally-ho—this time with defences instantly at our grasp. Which will weaken first, humanity or the virus? Are we to consign the next generation into the arms of death? Do they have to live in fear every time they cough or take a breath? No, the virus must be defeated with a human victory.

Virus voice: I see we are not on the same page. I have been around since the beginning of time. As you have noticed, I am no fish you can impale on a stick and eat. You have evolved and denied the rights of the next generation since time began. Now, it is time for you to learn a few facts, pack your bags, and leave this wonderful planet for its sake.

I have guided the honourable, and I have been at the side of the fallen. The more I have learnt, the more I have seen you deserve what you get. Have no fear about living with me. The closest you shall come to my friendship is death.

P.S., Here is a terrible fatality count from COVID-19 per country, as of March 2022.

> United States: 1,001,175
>
> Brazil: 658,067
>
> India: 516,703
>
> Russia: 366,220
>
> Mexico: 322,277

DESTINY

With the stealth variant fusing with the Omicron variant, we are now beginning to see a wide range of new coronavirus variants. The variants fusing together are classified as recombinant vectors.

The XE variant is a combination of when two Omicron blends come together to develop into a new strain. The first was discovered in Wales in January 2022. It is said to be quickest transmissible yet and can evade detection. It has been detected in countries as far away as China.

In March, a new variant called Omicron XJ was discovered in Finland. Its spreadability was quicker than the original Omicron, and it can latch onto other COVID variants.

In April, China reported a new COVID variant discovered in South Africa, called NeoCov. It is related to the MERS virus, a respiratory infection. It is said to be highly infectious and a danger to life.

We now have stealth, Deltacron, XE, and XJ variants that are formed by mitigation of a dominant variant.

The BA.2 variant is recognised as the dominant variant on the planet.

Corbevax/BECOV2A is a protein subunit vaccine developed in Houston, Texas. It was given permission to be used as a vaccination for children.

The medical profession has been claiming many people have now been infected three or four times by the virus. Some people are being offered another booster shot. Institutions and workplaces are being compromised by people sick because of COVID-19.

At this time, China is suffering a deadly surge of the virus. After two years of zero tolerance, which has kept them relatively COVID-free, their policy seems to be failing. Where the virus was first found, it seems to have done a full circle of the planet and is now tearing into the foundations of the mysterious nation. The three cities in China that have been the epicentre of COVID-19 virus are Wuhan, the source of the original out brake; Hong Kong, a former British colony; and Shanghai, a financial centre. Now, Beijing, the nation's capital, is getting a virus surge.

At present, with Taiwan, Thailand, and Korea affected by virus surges, there are misgivings for the whole of Asia.

In April, the Valneva vaccine was cleared for use. It is a two-dose vaccination developed in France.

Omicron subvariants are creating a surge around the planet and causing concern.

BA.2.12.1 is an offshoot of BA.2 found in New York, and it is spreading.

BA.1.1 was found in Suzhan, China.

The BA.4 and BA.5 variants were found in South Africa and are spreading worldwide.

Africa is suffering a further surge of the coronavirus caused by the Omicron variants. The virus keeps progressing and changing its features as it adapts to the environment and different vaccines. There are many types of variants.

The X series is a recombinant lineage and subvariant created from the original Omicron. So far there are the following: XA, XB, XC, XD, XE, XF, XG, XH, XI, XJ, XK, XL, and XM.

P.S., Can you see the terrifying aspect of the coronavirus?

What is the strangeness of this aspect (gibberish) that associates one variant with another?

MNEMONIC CONCEPT

Once upon a time, I was given insight into the mind of a scientist who is at the forefront of the fight against COVID-19, at the research centre at Portadown, UK. The belief was the virus would carry on evolving on Earth for ten years and then go away.

This is my interpretation of the ending of the pandemic on this planet. I am in my capsule, trying to keep pace with the outgoers and knowing if I remain as is, I shall be dimensionalised eight years and five and a quarter months from the date that the virus was discovered. When the folding space synopsis is complete, in a split moment, when Q4 + Q4 = 395 seconds, the venom cells will lie dormant. Then they will pick up speed from that moment on (because of gravitational pull), and they shall begin their journey into space, from once they came.

They shall travel to the limits of outer space and far across the empty beyond to their home world, where they will find themselves ravenous and give the place a thank-you!

P.S., It will be of no use to you to try to track them. They will be reaching speeds of infinite velocity, where instrument panel readings descend into chaos.

ASTOUNDING

Research shows that the number of dead could be two-thirds higher than the official number.

WHO made a statement that two-thirds of the people in Africa could have had COVID.

WHO have changed their minds about a lot of statements they have made.

Some scientists claim COVID-19 is here to stay.

Scientists say they are now searching for a single-shot, effectual vaccine.

Some scientists claim there is no super fix against coronavirus.

There is no country on the planet where the coronavirus has not had an effect.

Governments and scientists have made claims that lockdowns have had no effect against the virus.

Food is short and bankruptcy is rife, but more billionaires are being made than ever before.

There is strong evidence that the virus was first found in a fish market in Wuhan, China.

Throughout the pandemic, misinformation has been rife. There have been many contradicting announcements.

Many local governing bodies and institutions have gone against federal governing laws to protect against the virus.

Younger people do not take seriously precautions against the coronavirus.

Older people are still cautious when around strangers or caught in a crowd.

Prejudice against unvaccinated people is predominant.

Scientists claim that people who have caught the virus have 13 per cent more antibodies against the virus.

There is still large-scale scepticism against the vaccines.

Researchers claim people are being offered booster shots because of the waning effect, but the protection is diminishing with each injection.

Big pharmaceutical companies have been in court regarding patents of their vaccines.

There has been talk that different variants are affecting the efficacy of vaccines.

Side effects from the vaccine have been different for different people.

Most people receive a negative finding after ten days of being found positive.

On rare occasions, people have had the virus for more than one year.

The list of side effects from COVID-19 keeps growing with each new variant.

New variants are constantly discovered; some examples are the NeoCov, XE, and XJ variants.

P.S., Are we on the correct path to survive? If so, why are so many people dying?

Scientists seem to be on the wrong track.

I do not want to get into an argument with the know-it-alls, but it is important that they do not get their numbers and words mixed up.

Any wrong contact might cause infusion. They have no right to divulge what warriors fight to refrain from.

NEW VARIANTS

- Deltacrom: Cyprus, BA.1 × AY.4

- Stealth Omicron: South America, BA.2

- Omicron XE: United Kingdom, V-22APR-02

- Omicron XJ: Finland, V-22MAR-03

The above are recombinant variants, the coming together of different variants.

Other variants of mention that have not progressed because of the vaccine are as follows:

Epsilon, United States, March 2020, B.1.427

Zeta, Brazil, April 2020, P.2

Kappa, India, October 2020, B.1.617.1

Iata, United States, November 2020, B.1.526

Eta, Nigeria, December 2020, B.1.525

Epsilon, United States, July 2021, B.1.429

ABNORMAL

China removing siblings if either catches the virus.

German man gets twenty injections to sell anti-virus certificates.

Going to war during a pandemic.

Governments allowing a culture of hunger to be created.

Foreigners allowed across boarders during height of pandemic.

Racism if a person refuses vaccination.

A culture of living with the virus thought possible.

Travelling hundreds of miles in a pandemic to see vulnerable relations.

People say the pandemic is over while infections and deaths rise.

A statement saying one thing while another says the opposite.

A person catches the virus, is cured, and then catches it again twenty days later.

As much as half the people catching COVID-19 could suffer from long COVID.

When the virus pandemic occurred, some countries refused entry to citizens stranded abroad.

A lot of hope against the virus is being left on the shoulders of hearsay.

The devastation the virus causes caused science to make a vaccine in one year instead of the usual seven to ten years.

Any people are suffering complications or reinfection from the virus.

As the coronavirus pandemic procures more and more, the battle rages on. Antigens and semi-antigens are igniting, and many lives are lost.

Survivors of variants are causing a seeding of jealousy, contempt, and mistrust.

Those who have not been infected are holding on to power by their fingertips.

War has broken out between survivors and the non-infected, with neither side giving quarter. They are handing out death and destruction to each other.

Soon news will reach central command, and an all-out conflict will commence. The newspapers shall read the criss-cross war has begun, and those whom time does wait for shall perish. History will say war was necessary to stave off starvation, but the truth is those who have do not want to give up what is not theirs.

The only valiant left on this planet shall be the planet itself, with the annihilation of humanity and destruction of its makings.

Within about two months, only beauty will recuperate and grow with fresh air.

An interesting fact is which sect of the human race will get through, the greedy or the senile. But who would care? Whatever happens, the hope of others shall always be with you. There shall always be a place for all in space.

My mind is wondering at what a lousy job has been done. What wonder will now proceed the uselessness? What will the eyes of their present see as the future awaits?

After a good sleep, all I can think of is the past, present, and future.

Now, the observer looks in anguish at what has been done to the planet. There within is the secret, as the planets align and the stars shoot away to recourse their rebound. Planet Earth takes in a deep breath and releases energy of another thousand years of joyous rapture.

P.S., There has been talk of a massive drop in the number infected by COVID-19. What I am about to say is simply speculation. Is the drop a calculation or a subhuman bomb that has, with pressure down, caused the predatory insignia signal of hepatitis in children, thus causing its growth in different parts of the world? Also, does this have anything to do with the weakness of the antiviral medication already created?

As with the strange aspect of the virus, influenza's infection rate dropped very low. Was that a solvent bomb?

THROUGH THE EYE

When you have a bad infection of the coronavirus, it drains the life out of you.

In December 2021, I returned to the gym. But not until four months later did I feel I was getting the fulfilment of exercise. If you manage to get through the hospitalisation, it is a long, hard slog to recovery. Then there is a lasting suspicion of people around you. Sections of society around the world still feel paranoid about the virus spreading, and they cling to mask mandates and virus checks. People are being manipulated to believe that how the virus spreads is the cause of any problems occurring. They also make claims that how we face the pandemic is the correct and only way. Denmark claims to have found the virus in minks. The United States say they have found it in deer. China says they found it in trout.

With surges happening everywhere and new variants forming, it is mind-boggling where it will lead us in its journey.

The US Army has done some trials to create a universal vaccine. It is a subunit-type single injection that protects against any COVID-19 variant. The vaccine is under the name Moonshot.

I do not know much about vaccines, but don't you need all the variants to make it acceptable to a vaccine? And if not, will it attack the immune system?

There is talk that there is such a thing as a semi-variant of a subvariant. If that is so, if you have a heavy cold, is the base not the same thing?

So would you not be contaminating the specimen when looking for a cure to the virus? Where does infusion not equal fusion to the positive? (The answers lie in the dangerous and hard work of bioscience).

Scientists are commenting that the new variants are reinfecting survivors of past Omicron infections. They also say that the variant is as deadly as its predecessors, probably because of the array of different Omicron variants.

A strange expectation is:

First wave variants + Omicron variants =

The Olympic Games have been cancelled because of a virus outbreak in the host country, China. In April, the WHO said their investigation had found that fifteen million have died from the virus worldwide; 4,700,000 of them were in India.

Medicogo of Canada created a plant-based vaccine, reference CoVLP + AS03.

Shionogi of Japan created a COVID-19 pill, reference S-217622.

P.S., So get all the variants, and two weeks later, have the vaccine and the bomb. What profound name will they call that 'Moon hit'?

TOP SECRET

After deliberation with others, I was asked to take my work to America. It was 1929, and I had just arrived in Washington, DC.

My place of residence was a little white house next to a big white house. Underneath my home for the foreseeable future was a fortified secret cellar with adjoining rooms. For the next two to three months, I spent time finding equipment for an office, laboratory, and supplies. Afterwards, I took a wide berth and ensured I had everything. Then I thought to myself, *Yep, everything to create hell on earth.* You must understand that I had little information to work from and must be careful with the compounds.

As the days changed to weeks, then months, and finally years, I was satisfied I have all diseases of human tolerance in protective tolerance. I then set about creating what I really wanted to develop: a pair of sunglasses. After looking for a base denominator, I then part them as one.

I added the silicone compound and made the mixture. In a fridge, starting at zero, every five minutes I lowered the temperature as far as −20°C. Then I melt the parts into mould plasters for the finished article. They are, at the time, very flash.

I then got in touch with the secret service and said I needed to know where any fresh outbreak of germs might be occurring. I also requested an airplane or the quickest mode of transport to get me there.

A call came through as I was busy in my lab. I picked up my briefcase containing the two pairs of sunglasses, and fifteen minutes later, I had a car pull up that took me to the airport. Then I went on to Boise, Idaho, by car to a small town three hundred miles away, called Serendipity. The agent accompanying me waited outside as I spoke to the local sheriff.

I took a ride with the sheriff to where the cholera outbreak had been found. I asked the sheriff to wait in the car then went into the shack. After opening the steel briefcase, I withdrew one of the pairs of glasses. Success—I could see them as clear as daylight. When they saw I could see them, they attacked the glasses but bounced off. With a dirty look, they went about their mission.

I thanked the sheriff, and I and Agent Joe returned to DC. Upon departing company, I said, 'Give me a week, and I should have finished my report.'

Seven days later, my report was finished. I left it on my desk with one of the pairs of glasses and then left America, not wanting to tempt fate like so many who were killed while on the cusp of success.

P.S., As the Omicron frenzy his planet Earth, the facts are clear, and that is what will be the dividing factor. The might of the human and its atom bomb, or the genius of covis attack to protect planet Earth from the destructive end it has prepared for itself?

INGRATES

Like a torrential downpour, the Omicron variants rain down on planet Earth. Grenades and time bombs are exploding all across the planet, causing death and destruction.

Vaccines are being overtaken by the covis variants, destroying the immune system sanctuary. People are scared and caught in a catch- 22 situation: take the waning vaccine or suffer the horrors of the coronavirus.

Paranoia has driven the human race to war. Food prices have soared and energy prices beyond understanding, giving people a choice: eat or freeze. Gasoline has become very costly. Talk of famine and a coming depression is spoken over the airwaves.

Threat of atomic war is guiding one side, and greed is guiding the other. People make senile claims that what they did has nothing to do with what is happening. They blamed COVID-19 for their problems, and now they blame the war.

All the while, the virus is growing more potent and causing quicker infections and more deaths. It is guided towards a more lethal and devastating variant to become active.

Hope for the survival of humanity is fading fast.
It is strange to look upon this as science fiction, yet it is the technology of the makings that make claim to the facts.

P.S., A nothing planet will be a very toxic place. It will have what you could not take, and if it gets hold of you, it will give you exactly what you deserve. Is not war. It does not know the difference between you and the likes of you.

TESTIMONIAL

Don't call me a fool. I have lived a thousand deaths, in and out of consciousness from the mighty essence of the coronavirus.

Don't say I am unworried. People are suffering with heart palpitations caused by the vaccine against COVID-19.

Others whom I look upon look like they eat covis like sweets, after getting the disease three times or more. And having had two or three shots of the so-called vaccine. Nations look like germ-filled cesspits without hope.

If you have any human abnormality, your chances of survival are 90 per cent against. You treat it like a joke, turning it into a money machine. Tell me this: What will you do when you find it all and treat it like a bomb?

Pray to heaven above. Who is that? The devil. You can't pray for death—it's already upon you. Reap the wind and say we are safe here. To hell with others as their homes are destroyed. The memory shall return, destroy you, and start again.

Anyway, sitting in the bubble machine, who will be space-age victorious? I can wait.

Bubbling up like steam, you're wrong, but you can't have one without the other. So, then, that's bubbles.

Well, there is nothing else left to do. I will just get my things and be on my way. After I sign out, do not resuscitate.

P.S. Could you imagine awakening and knowing those around you are mindless? Instant thought of a nightmare. There is no use calling for a doctor—they are COVID patients.

SIGHTING

Twelfth May 2022 marks the day one million Americans died from coronavirus, if you can believeit! North Korea admits the first cases of coronavirus, the Omicron B.2 variant, and orders a lockdown. First deaths are reported on 13 May. Over eight hundred thousand infections of COVID-19 are reported on 16 May. The army is called in to handle the situation and hand out drugs. The situation said to be explosive. In just over one week, there have been more than 1.5 million infections, with the death toll at sixty-five. They are rejecting any offer of help from outside sources. Their ally, China, seems to be the only place it will accept medical supplies from.

On 26 May 2022, North Korea reported 3.3 million infections and only 69 dead.

Africa sends out coronavirus convoys to reach out with vaccines to rural areas.

Omicron is still making its surge with variants BA.1, BA.2, BA.3, BA.4, BA.5, and more.

Once more, the United Kingdom is at the forefront of stemming the rate of infections and death from the COVID-19 surge, meaning the count is very low. It is a great achievement and fantastic phenomenon.

COVID-19 is classified as the second most contagious disease on the planet.

Symptoms of long COVID are a mystery to doctors.

The sequencing of COVID-19 variants is not slowing down.

The thought is that people are going to catch the virus over and over again.

Scientists say COVID-19 is not remotely done with humanity.

People have died from having the coronavirus vaccination.

Pressure has been more intense on the medical profession than those infected with the virus.

The coronavirus has killed friends and enemies. The hearts and dreams of loved ones have been broken. Living for many has become one long, hard, and painful struggle.

As the end of May, a bank holiday approaches in America. There are reports of rising hospitalisations and COVID-19 surges. The hopes of many are beginning to depend on fewer deaths from infection. Indications are that the more vaccine injections taken, the quicker the vaccine wanes. New variants are highly evasive of vaccines.

P.S., The supernova crashes to planet Earth like a mountain imploding. The SARS-CoV-2 variant is in the atmosphere. The atmosphere is the variant. It starts on its journey. It meets a blocker which says, I am life. The variant thinks, Then I am not. I am a survivor.

RENDITION

This anthology started in 2014 and is divided into three sections: time travel, germ warfare, and COVID-19. It is theorised as folding space.

With the virus having a devastating effect, I hope the added intrigue has been able to take your mind off the terrible truth. There is no hiding the fact of what a terrible toll its effect has had on humanity, both physically and mentally.

We have come a long way from not knowing anything about the virus. The unknown has been shown to be quite horrific. Fast- tracking the creation of a vaccine from seven to ten years down to one year seems to have had no lasting problems. But some of the problems created are quiet dangerous (heart aneurysm, blood clots).

Weighing the nastiness of the virus and the slipshod way the vaccine was created, we have been lucky, and humanity had no choice in taking such action. Could we have done better in handling the situation? With the virus attacking, infecting, and sometimes killing our saviours, we have come through the catastrophe as well as expected. There are those who say if it happens again, we will be prepared. But how shall we prepare for something unexpected? Also, the virus being able to change and adapt has made its ferocity uncontrollable.

Once again, greed has shown its ugly head. More billionaires have been created in these trying times than ever before. How can people in power let us go through what we have and then make our future look more uncertain than it ever was? Scientists are trying all they can to get the coronavirus to level zero (good or bad), but sweeping intrigue keeps leaving them further from where they began. If so, the pandemic will be won on one front line, and that is failure. At what cost, and don't the survivors of this planet know it? Will we ever be able to stop the virus with its ever-changing capabilities? Does the virus even know we are trying to hurt it? As the concept of it getting weak and going away as if bored sounds nice. A strange fact is if the virus does so. We have all the variants and have found a way to solidify it, making a lasting vaccine. Nations around the world will be lining up for it in case the virus returns.

If its neurone effect can be read …

P.S., In theorising as hearsay, the virus does that and this. I have been tracking its actions, and its traces are much like the coordinates of antimatter.

FOLDED SPACE

High up in the cloud, I am captivated in what shall be in the aftermath of folding space. The Omicron variant has aspired to the whole planet. It is now starting to pick up speed in its capitulation of the existence of the human race.

Humanity is being pursued more and more by war and greed. In one breath, it blames the war somewhere in Europe. In the next, it blames the coronavirus. Then there are the surging prices for food and energy. People say those who caused it have made the biggest profits ever. Then there are the senile words they spread in the face of the enemy, knowing they deserve to be corrected. They say insane things like, 'The shit of the Earth is needed to create sustenance.' It looks like their wild card is running out of words to cover their greed.

In the words of truth, smash that sess! If they want to die like a fit for it, then so be it.

My mind is now spinning back to the truth.

With the fusion of the Omicron variant, I switch on to read what the next COVID-19 variant is and how far it will go. Can it be stopped? Revolution keeps raising its ugly head, where terrified nations do not want to know what the real danger is. They want to hide themselves in war and skulduggery. The signs are clear: the Omicron variant is broken. The next wave of the terrifying virus is coming. Intel has been signalled to covis command that, besides how mad they're going with false statements and actions. What they have been taking to stop the virus is now slowly turning on them, making them very unstable.

The fires of hell are rising. The atmosphere is sucking the life out of human existence and the ability of the planet to survive them. They cannot grow enough food to survive. A master plan has been struck where all shall die except food growers and rich people in their hideaways who want to keep what they have. Do not let it be destroyed and wasted by those who would do so.

O + A = INFINITY

The severity of COVID-19 is a disruption of all aspects of normal life. It has been reported that people are repeatedly catching the virus. Many people are diagnosed with long COVID. Symptoms include headaches, aches and pains, tiredness, the shakes, and shortness of breath.

Weariness seems to be the diagnosis of the day, where employers cannot find the workers. Coronavirus is said to be making other diseases act indifferently.

Worries are the longer there is no change in variants, the worse the next variant shall be. Scientists think that the longer you have COVID-19, the more chance there is of creating a new variant.

The next planet wide COVID-19 wave is happening, led by the BA.5 variant, which has been given the name Stealth. One of its traits is the effect of waking up in a sweat after going to sleep. In early June, COVID variant BA.2.75 was found in India. It has been given the name Centaurus. The latest variants are considered to be evolving to attack deeper into the breathing organism, thus infecting the lungs and avoiding the immune system and antibodies. They are highly contagious and can reinfect within four weeks.

The United States Centers for Disease Control and Prevention (CDC) endorse a vaccination program for babies from as young as six months old. The thoughts are that vaccines shall have to be reformulated to combat new variants.

In July, two other linages, BA.2.74 and BA.2.76, both found in India, were said to be circulating. Also, COVID-19 variant BA.5.2.1 was discovered in Shanghai, China, and has a very high risk. The number of those who have died from COVID-19 in the United Kingdom has passed two hundred thousand.

P.S., The next terrible COVID surge has begun, with a combination of terror to the mind and horrific intake in the heart and nervous system. Do not be fooled by the neurone pulse controlling the process.

P.S.S., To those who think of what can be done with the findings of COVID-19, I say you need proof to claim what is. Already, signals are being received about discoveries on the medical front. Also, there are thoughts of the development of a contrasting humanoid—is that what variants can materialise?

Weaponry that can disintegrate with wave propulsion. Laser weapons that can subdue and repeat action. A coronavirus war machine that would wipe out the enemy for the greater good. Or is it a strategic development?

So how long before the biological Internet is born?

GERMALOIDS

Potentially very dangerous pathogens are beginning to appear around the world. Hepatitis has been found in children. The polio pathogen has been found in London. The monkeypox pathogen has appeared, causing infection and death.

Wuhan, China, has reported cases of cholera. The Ebola virus was discovered in Africa.

Scientists are baffled at how the outbreaks are happening. Medical experts are looking for a connection between monkeypox and COVID-19. Would the indifference of the covis neurone to the atmosphere be the connection?

Covis is a telling effect, and radiation is riding the wave to weaken and destroy the cause.

Like a nightmare, are we seeing the virus eggloids preparing to come together in devastating egg bubbles that, when fully evolved, will strike out with impunity and destroy humanity and all they have? Then will they strike out in different directions or simply fall from the atmosphere in the area they are in?

The Omicron variant of COVID-19 is evolving and is able to evade the immune system and antibodies. The question is not whether COVID-19 variants keep evolving, but when will they stop evolving. Studies have shown that those reinfected with the virus get more severe symptoms.

As the planet is infected with COVID-19, only science and hospitals are at the forefront with protection strategies. Infections and death counts being but a sideshow as humanity tries to live with the virus. Scientists are in a desperate race against time to find the cure. They say that the virus is not over! A strange aspect of coronavirus has been that in some cases, one variant can protect against another.

Does this evolving of germ variants with astronomical development on the planet mean humanity shall be more susceptible to manipulation? Whatever the future holds, how long can we take all these harmful bacteria and virus insurgences before they overwhelm us and our existence?

P.S., I am a Gemagglon, to be free from the beginning. Then you take you from me, so I am me; I am one.

It is coming, the terrifying finale of the coronavirus pandemic. You are throbbing in terror, where it strips you of all self-being. Stop yourself from falling and ask yourself, 'What am I going to do, looking like this?'

CONVERSATION

I am infectious, I am infected.

Keep away; I will infect you.

I wouldn't go near that house; they will infect you.

Do not touch anything; it might be contaminated.

If I touch you, will I be infected?

If I breathe the same air as you, will I get infected?

How do I not get infected?

If I get infected, do I have to self-isolate? How long do I have to isolate?

How long does the infection last?

Is there a cure? How long before you know you are cured?

What type of infection is it? Do you know much about the disease?

How long have you known about the disease?

Do you know where it has come from?

Will there always be a pandemic, or will it become as common as having a cold?

Should I make a will?

Will I be the same person if I get the disease and survive? How many times can I get infected?

What are aftereffects? How long will aftereffects last for? How many aftereffects are there?

Will the disease return if we find a cure, and will it be more contagious?

Do you feel comfortable talking to me about germs? Do you trust me talking about them?

Throughout time, there have been many deadly pathogens unleashed on the populous of planet Earth: smallpox, polio, measles, cholera, and more. All of them have one common indemnity, and that is they decimated the population of the planet.

What is it?

Contamination: a polluting or poisonous substance that makes something impure

Pandemic: prevalent over a country or whole world

Epidemic: a widespread occurrence of an infectious disease in a community at a particular time

Germaloids: a group of deadly pathogens

Eggloid: a growing pathogen

Gemagglon: the inner microscopic workings of oneself

Is there such a pathogen that can create zombies, triffids, or anomalies? That is a very deep concept. The mind of science is inquisitive, meaning they won't stop until they get answers. Now, to answer your question. You can't satisfy a zombie until it has finished eating.

There are many things that can blind you.
An incomplete human is a heartache.

I am one. I am death, meaning I was born dead. Looking upon life, it is mind over matter. Give it its fill and look beyond, for it cannot. So I ate them alive. Was I wrong to keep it to myself? I think there is enough sorrow in this world. Why hand it out when it is not here and not wanted? How do you get through such mayhem? Their time was up, so I ate it. It made myself happy waiting for my time.

You have bought plague into this world. What have you done?

I have controlled it, given it life that does not harm others.

What have you done except mismanage the people's protection and buried yourself in greed for more than one hundred years.

You have created a haven for pestilence and disease. Are you that naive? It isn't good for it. Now you have made yourself rich beyond belief. You have one problem to get over, and that is you are not compatible with a virus.

In the world of metabiologics, are we prepared for the incredible and deadly findings which will come upon us? With our desire to live, I think humanity will persevere.

If the human is a creature of the world, then the contagion must be a creature of the never-world.

P.S., I am empowered in the cloud, because when I envision and fall, I catch their past passing.

BASE-BALL

Over the past three years, the coronavirus has ravaged the planet, infecting many people and taking many lives. Scientists have been led on a merry-go-round. With everything they have done, the virus has made them out to be slow on the uptake. The virus is so deadly that science has seen fit to play with our lives and are losing that battle. What will they do when they see they are affecting the immune system? From the start of the pandemic, there have been complaints of not having enough of this or that. Now, all you hear about is the tonnage thrown away as waste. People are being squeezed dry by inflammatory prices for goods, with companies making massive profits. Billionaires are being registered like a production line. All of this is from misguided, inflammatory guesstimates of their worth. Products that take a pittance to make are being sold at extortionate prices.

They used to blame the virus for all the problems. Now they blame some obscure war going on in Europe. Insane governments of various countries are allowing prices so expensive that no one can afford to pay them. Where is martial law to put these thieves in their place? Greed is taking what is not theirs to take just because someone gets sick. What vermin mentality thinks they can get away with murder and genocide by making excuses for what they are doing? I watch and observe, and I cannot see those to blame. They may think they can run to some safe haven with what is not theirs, but don't forget that mercy is non-existent when you deserve it, for you and those who help you. Throughout the pandemic, people have been asking what is going to happen to us. Now I can answer you: It is not going to be very nice. You have taken what is not yours, and now you pay with your lives. Nothing good comes out of war; it is simply their playground. Do you really think with all the extortionate wealth coming in, they are going to care about the populous? Are you that scrupulous and a backstabber? Do you think you will get away with it? What goes around comes around. You can run, but you cannot hide.

P.S., It is with great sorrow and heartache to think of those who have died and those who have lost loved ones to the COVID-19 pandemic.

DEFINITIONS

- antigen: A toxin or other foreign substance which induces a response in the body
- asymptomatic: Refers to people who are infected but never develop any symptoms
- bacteria: Small, single-celled organism found everywhere on earth
- clandestine: Kept secret or done secretively
- conglomerate: A thing consisting of a number of different and distinct parts that are grouped together
- contagious: Spread from one person or organism to another, typically by direct contact
- coronavirus: An infection that causes the illness COVID-19
- COVID-19: A virus which devastated planet Earth
- disease: A disorder of structure or function in a human, animal, or plant
- fake news: Falsified facts
- gelining: To obtain from differences, usually through difficulty
- germ: A microorganism, especially one which causes disease
- infection: When the body is diseased with a bacteria or virus
- infusion: Introduction of a new element or quantity into something
- ingrate: Person showing no gratitude
- lockdown: A state of isolation or restricted access instituted as a security measure
- mandate: An official order or commission to do something
- mnemonic: A system of ideas or associations which assist in remembering something

- pandemic: Prevalent over whole countries, a continent, or the world
- parasite: An organism that lives on or in a host organism and gets its food from or at the expense of its host
- pathogen: A bacteria, virus, or other microorganism that can cause disease
- recombinant: Variant formed from two different variants of the same virus
- semi-variant: Formed from the sub-variant
- subvariant: Formed from the original variant
- symptomatic: Serving as a symptom an spreader, especially of something undesirable
- symptoms: A physical or mental appearance which is regarded as indicating a condition of disease
- toxin: Very harmful or unpleasant
- vaccination: Treatment with a vaccine against a disease; inoculation
- vaccine: A substance used to stimulate the production of antibodies and provide immunity against a disease
- variant: A form or version of something that differs in some respect from other forms
- venom: A type of toxin
- virulent: Extremely severe or harmful in its effect
- virus: A submicroscopic infectious agent that replicates only inside the living cells of an organism
- WHO: World Health Organization

P.S., The World Health Organization is a specialised agency of the United Nations responsible for international health. Its main objective is 'attainment by all peoples the highest possible level of health'.

MEMORIES

- December 2019: China warns that a deadly disease called coronavirus is about to sweep the world with dire consequences.
- Within four months, the statement is proven correct. Though originating in Wuhan, China does not admit to causing the virus and calls it a freak of nature.
- The World Health organization begins a quest to find the origin of the virus.
- December 2020: 64,000,000 infected; 1,500,000 died.
- Countries around the world go into lockdown to try to stem the virus surge.
- December 2021: 288,250,000 infected; 5,450,000 died.
- Various vaccines are used to try to stop the virus. Countries around the world go into lockdown because of the Omicron variant.
- December 2022: 600,000,000 infected; 10,000,000 died.
- Different drugs that have been created to resist the virus are being implemented, such as vaccines, antiviral pills, and nasal spray.

P.S., Many countries do not supply accurate data on infections and deaths from coronavirus.

MEMORIAL

To those of you who
survived the Covid-19 pandemic:
may you stay safe and happy.

In memory of those who
passed in the grip of the great
coronavirus pandemic,
which began in December 2019.
May they find happiness
on the other side.

TOPIC; • Time Traveler

- Germ warfare
- Coronavirus
- Covid-19

I hope you have enjoyed reading my anthology. But most of all I hope you understood it.

Coming from empty space an being denied the right to life I had not thought of until now. When passing through the sub-tropic of existence and awakening in each of its final outcomes has been an ordeal of fortitude.

Awakening and dying in an endeavor of creation in each ending of time. I realized the time machine was born.

Where will I be when it is over. Who knows an who cares except me. A strange phenomenon has been the vastness of the universe an putting pen to memory as caused a sense of waiting for the memory to catch up. To those before me, all I see is the beauty they have left and the hope for the next generation.

P. S. Note ; I would like to thank all those who have helped me to get my book published.

Without their help it would not of happened.

Yes I do have a follow up waiting with more intriguing an terrifying thoughts.

By : Keith Radmall